T0199148

Better than Gold

*HOW MUCH BETTER TO GET
WISDOM THAN GOLD!*

PROVERBS 16:16

WRITTEN BY KEVIN MILLER
WITH JENN MILLER

WESTBOW
PRESS®
A DIVISION OF THOMAS NELSON
& ZONDERVAN

Copyright © 2018 Kevin Miller; Jenn Miller.

All rights reserved. No part of this book may be used or reproduced by any means, graphic, electronic, or mechanical, including photocopying, recording, taping or by any information storage retrieval system without the written permission of the author except in the case of brief quotations embodied in critical articles and reviews.

WestBow Press books may be ordered through booksellers or by contacting:

WestBow Press
A Division of Thomas Nelson & Zondervan
1663 Liberty Drive
Bloomington, IN 47403
www.westbowpress.com
1 (866) 928-1240

Because of the dynamic nature of the Internet, any web addresses or links contained in this book may have changed since publication and may no longer be valid. The views expressed in this work are solely those of the author and do not necessarily reflect the views of the publisher, and the publisher hereby disclaims any responsibility for them.

Any people depicted in stock imagery provided by Getty Images are models, and such images are being used for illustrative purposes only.
Certain stock imagery © Getty Images.

The Holy Bible, English Standard Version® (ESV®)
Copyright © 2001 by Crossway,
a publishing ministry of Good News Publishers.
All rights reserved.
ESV Text Edition: 2016

ISBN: 978-1-9736-3780-6 (sc)
ISBN: 978-1-9736-3779-0 (e)

Print information available on the last page.

WestBow Press rev. date: 09/12/2018

Contents

Intro... Page 1

Proverbs 1.. Page 4

Proverbs 2.. Page 8

Proverbs 3.. Page 12

Proverbs 4.. Page 16

Proverbs 5.. Page 20

Proverbs 6.. Page 24

Proverbs 7.. Page 28

Proverbs 8.. Page 32

Proverbs 9.. Page 36

Proverbs 10.. Page 40

Proverbs 11.. Page 44

Proverbs 12.. Page 48

Proverbs 13.. Page 52

Proverbs 14.. Page 56

Proverbs 15.. Page 60

Proverbs 16.. Page 64

Proverbs 17.. Page 68

Proverbs 18.. Page 72

Proverbs 19.. Page 76

Proverbs 20 .... Page 80

Proverbs 21.. Page 84

Proverbs 22 .... Page 88

Proverbs 23.. Page 92

Proverbs 24.. Page 96

Proverbs 25.. Page 100

Proverbs 26.. Page 104

Proverbs 27.. Page 108

Proverbs 28.. Page 112

Proverbs 29 .... Page 116

Proverbs 30 .... Page 120

Proverbs 31.. Page 124

About the Authors .... Page 128

About Awaken Church.. Page 129

Acknowledgements .... Page 131

Contents

Intro

Have you ever held a brick of gold? You know, like the gold bricks in the bank heist movies. I've never held one, but I've always wanted to. The weight of the brick, the shimmer of its finish, its inherent value—it's all so intriguing. Criminals in movies and in real life go to great lengths to acquire the gold, knowing it will change their lives.

What if we viewed God's Word in a similar light? Its weightiness, its value, and its ability to change our lives are intriguing. Spiritually speaking, when you hold God's Word, it's as if you are holding a gold mine of wisdom, knowledge, and direction.

Actually, gold doesn't even compare to the eternal value of God's Word. God's Word is *better than gold!*

Wisdom is something everyone is after in some way. Whenever we try to learn more, lead better, streamline something, or excel in an area or craft, we are seeking wisdom. Proverbs 16:16 says it is better to get wisdom than gold! That's quite the statement. A brick of gold could go a long way, but God's Word will go much further.

Job, Psalms, Proverbs, Ecclesiastes, and Song of Solomon are often referred to as "wisdom literature." These books are written in poetic language, containing a gold mine of wisdom and guidance for the Christian life. As you work at developing a habit of daily time in God's Word, I suggest reading a Proverb each day. Since there are thirty-one chapters in Proverbs and seven of the twelve months have thirty-one days, it's easy to remember which Proverb to read each day. I hope you find this book useful and applicable, but most importantly, I hope it gives you a greater appreciation of and hunger for God's Word.

Here are five things that will be helpful as you discipline yourself to spend time daily in God's Word...

PLAN

Studies show that you are much more prone to work out in the morning if you set out your workout clothes and shoes the night before. The same is true for your time with the Lord. You won't *have* time to spend in God's Word; you need to *make* time. I recommend having a place in your house (office, living room chair, back porch) where you frequent, as well as a reading plan that will help you stay on track with reading the Bible. Be strategic. Staying focused on God's Word will not happen accidentally.

PAGES

I love technology and I regularly recommend using Bible apps for your phone, tablet, and computer. However, one thing I've learned about myself is how easily distracted I am when technology is in the room. An actual paper Bible isn't the only way to read, but I recommend it as a way to keep you focused. Find a translation of the Bible you enjoy reading (The English Standard Version, New Living Translation, and the New International Version are all great), then dive into the pages of God's Word every day.

PEN

We've all read something—maybe even most of a book—then realized we have no idea what we just read. Having a pen in hand may not seem like a big deal but for me, it's very important. Having a pen ready to underline, circle, and make notes within my Bible is key to keeping me focused. Staying focused on underlining important words and phrases helps keep my brain and heart engaged, and helps in my fight against forgetfulness. I regularly write things down in my journal that God spoke to me through His Word.

PRAYER

It's fun to meet your favorite author and get a quick signature and a handshake but honestly, it's normally quick and impersonal. Here's some really good news: every day you are first in line to talk to the Author of the Bible. God Himself, who made sure the words of Scripture were penned for our benefit, tells us to "with confidence draw near to the throne of grace, that we may receive mercy and find grace to help in time of need" (Hebrews 4:16). There are no crowds to fight, lines to stand in, or pushy security guards. You are the only one who stands in your way of talking to the Author through prayer! Before you open your Bible, ask God to speak to you through it, then keep the conversation rolling as you read.

PAUSE

Our culture is so focused on getting things done, checking off to-do lists, and moving at the speed of life that it's easy to rush through your time in God's Word. Remember, reading God's Word is about so much more than reading some words on a page (or a screen). Time in God's Word is about time with God, allowing Him to shape our lives and build on the foundation of our faith. God tells us that "ALL Scripture is breathed out by God and profitable..." (2 Timothy 3:16). In that case, every word is there on purpose and our job is to take the time to see how we can learn more about God through each word.

At the end of each chapter in this book, we have provided some questions to help you dig deeper into the gold mine of God's Word. We hope you use this book as a practical resource in your daily time with the Lord as you learn that God's Word is *Better Than Gold*.

Proverbs 1

GPS FOR YOUR SOUL

Google Maps saved my life. I guess not literally, but it feels like it sometimes. It's hard to remember the days before GPS when I had to look at a paper map or ask for directions from a human! After years of living in Clarksville, TN, I still often use Google Maps to get around.

I guess what I'm getting at is that *I've realized how necessary it is to receive direction.*

Proverbs is like Google Maps for your soul. It contains direction, warnings, hazards, rest stops along the way, and ultimately points us toward our final destination. The rewards of listening to and living by the wisdom found in this book are *better than gold!*

Proverbs chapters 1-9 are not actually the proverbs just yet. They are more of a chat from a father to his son.

Proverbs 1:1-7 define the purpose of the book, ending with this reminder:

> "THE FEAR OF THE LORD IS THE
> BEGINNING OF KNOWLEDGE; FOOLS
> DESPISE WISDOM AND INSTRUCTION."
> — PROVERBS 1:7 —

The fear of the Lord isn't about being frightened or terrified; it's about honor and reverence. The fear of the Lord comes from a posture of humility, understanding that God is the First and the Last, the Beginning and the End. The prophet Isaiah reminds us that God's ways and thoughts are higher than ours (Isaiah 55:8-9). That's good news because our ability to think, dream, and see what's ahead is extremely limited. The fear of the Lord means understanding that since God sees the whole picture, He is able to guide us safely and more accurately than we would ever be able to guide ourselves.

After all, as verse 7 reminds us, it is foolish to despise Godly wisdom and instruction. In case you were wondering how foolish it is, all you have to do is keep reading Proverbs 1. Those living in sin, who are all around us trying to entice us, are actually self-deceived. They think they're lying in wait for others, but Proverbs 1:18 says "these men lie in wait for their own blood; they set an ambush for their own lives." Verse 31 continues, "they shall eat the fruit of their way, and have their fill of their own devices."

Sin leads to a selfish, foolish, self-destructive life. Speaking of fear, it's frightening that God has given us free will—the ability to choose the path our lives will take. Thankfully, God has given us the path of wisdom to follow.

> **"WHOEVER LISTENS TO ME (WISDOM)**
> **WILL DWELL SECURE AND WILL BE AT**
> **EASE, WITHOUT DREAD OF DISASTER."**
> **— PROVERBS 1:33 —**

A faith-filled, wisdom-guided life is a life that doesn't have to fear the future. We live at ease, knowing there is no need to constantly "dread disaster." Disaster will come but thankfully, we know the God who will give us the wisdom and direction to overcome the worst disasters life throws at us!

Dig Deeper

1. Which verse in Proverbs 1 stood out to you most and why?

_____

_____

_____

_____

_____

_____

2. Since God's Word acts as a GPS for our souls, where are some areas you see are leading you away from where you want to be heading? How can you realign things and go God's way instead?

_____

_____

_____

_____

_____

_____

"

A FAITH-FILLED,
WISDOM GUIDED LIFE IS
A LIFE THAT DOESN'T HAVE
TO **FEAR THE FUTURE.**

Proverbs 2

ANTI-OSMOSIS

In school, I remember wishing I could learn school subjects through osmosis. If only learning biology was as easy as sleeping with a biology book under my pillow! Skipping late night cram sessions would be worth a few nights of uncomfortable sleep on a lumpy pillow. I learned that I couldn't pass geometry simply because I hung out with other kids who were good at math. It doesn't work that way. Knowledge—and in the context of Proverbs, wisdom—comes through an intentional pursuit.

Proverbs 2:2-4 reminds us to "make your ear attentive to wisdom...incline your heart to understanding...call out for insight...raise your voice for understanding...seek it...and search for it." In other words, you won't stumble over wisdom and understanding. It will take work to obtain it. *Wisdom won't find its way to your heart because your Bible found its way under your pillow.*

There are many men and women I admire for their Godly wisdom and knowledge of Scripture. I imagine you can think of a few examples as well. They didn't arrive there by accident. It took years of prayer, faithfulness, and intentionality to learn, grow in, and seek wisdom. Chances are that if you ask them about it, they'll be the first to admit (if they're actually wise!) they haven't arrived. They're still on a quest for Godly wisdom. It's a lifelong pursuit.

Although wisdom takes time and patience, Proverbs 2 is also a great reminder of the source and value of the pursuit.

"FOR THE LORD GIVES WISDOM;
FROM HIS MOUTH COME KNOWLEDGE
AND UNDERSTANDING;"
— PROVERBS 2:6 —

True wisdom can be found from no other source. Sure, read some books and study your subject of choice but true, Godly wisdom only comes from one source—the mouth of God. Thankfully, He's compiled His words into a book we call *the* Word!

Never stop pursuing it. The rest of Proverbs 2 reminds us of the value of the pursuit. Wisdom delivers us from the way of evil (verse 12), from lust (verse 16), and from its destructive consequences. If you will follow wisdom, "you will walk in the way of the good and keep to the paths of the righteous" (Proverbs 2:20).

So, let's put all the pieces together: wisdom that will preserve your soul and set you on a path of salvation from sin and blessing from God will only be found through an ongoing, intentional pursuit of the God who is the source of wisdom. In that case, what is slowing you down and how can you pursue Godly wisdom in a more intentional way? Whatever sacrifices you have to make will be worth it!

Dig Deeper

1. Which verse in Proverbs 2 stood out to you most and why?

_____

_____

_____

_____

_____

_____

2. What are some strategic ways you can begin being more intentional with your pursuit of God and His Word?

_____

_____

_____

_____

_____

_____

"

GODLY WISDOM ONLY COMES
FROM ONE SOURCE - THE MOUTH
OF GOD. THANKFULLY, HE'S COMPILED
HIS WORDS INTO A BOOK WE
CALL **THE WORD!**

Proverbs 3

TRUST FALL

A "trust fall" is where you stand on an elevated surface with your back to your friends and on their command, you simply fall backwards off the ledge, trusting they will catch you. YouTube clips prove this can often be a recipe for disaster!

But what if we upped the ante? What if instead of just your body, *everything* was on the line? Your finances, family, friends, and future? It turns out, it *IS* all on the line. Proverbs 3 gives us the answer and tells us *Who* to trust.

> "TRUST IN THE LORD WITH ALL YOUR
> HEART, AND DO NOT LEAN ON YOUR
> OWN UNDERSTANDING. IN ALL YOUR
> WAYS ACKNOWLEDGE HIM, AND HE
> WILL MAKE STRAIGHT YOUR PATHS."
> — PROVERBS 3:5-6 —

Here's a simplified translation of those verses: **Trust God with everything always!**

It's the trust fall times ten. Trust God with the direction of your life (verse 6), temptation (verse 7), the first and best of your finances (verse 9), discipline and pain (verse 11), and everything else. Unfortunately, the illusion of control can blind us to the truth that it's all out of our control.

Let's discuss this a little further in depth because *saying* you trust God is one thing, but *actually trusting Him* is another.

How do we trust God with the direction of our lives? We rest in the reality that He sees the whole picture when we see just a fraction of the picture. We see the pieces, but He sees the whole puzzle. *There is no need to fear the future when we know the One who holds the future!*

How do we trust God when we face temptation? We fight hard, knowing with every temptation comes a way of escape (1 Corinthians 10:13). We are not the victims of sin and temptation, we are more than conquerors (Romans 8:37), but fighting temptation is not easy. We trust that God's way is best even when it's the hardest.

How do we trust God with our finances? We recognize that "my" finances are not actually "my" finances. Your name may be on that paycheck but none of it is actually yours. God is the Provider and He demands and deserves our first and best. Trust Him with it and see if He won't bless you in response to your trust.

How do we trust God through discipline? As much as you may want to discipline that unruly kid you see in the grocery store, you had better keep your hands off! Discipline only comes from a loving parent. When you fail, take pleasure in the pain of discipline because it reminds you of your Father's love. He's just treating you as one of His own.

According to Proverbs 3, blessing comes through finding wisdom, and it's not just a little blessing either. Verses 14-15 remind us that the rewards of wisdom are better than the rewards that come from silver, gold, and precious jewels!

If the first half of Proverbs 3 is a trail map of how to trust God, the second half is a list of how not to do it (which can be equally helpful). Just as loving parents set up boundaries for their children to protect and guide them, God does the same for us. "Don't do this," "Don't say that," and "Don't live this way" are all God's ways of guiding our lives to be the best they can be. God knows that the best way to live our lives is to be completely devoted to Him.

Dig Deeper

1. Which verse in Proverbs 3 stood out to you most and why?

_____

_____

_____

_____

_____

_____

2. Of the topics we discussed (direction, temptation, finances, discipline), which is the hardest area for you to trust God in? What do you need to do to begin trusting Him more?

_____

_____

_____

_____

_____

_____

"

THERE IS NO NEED TO FEAR
THE FUTURE WHEN WE KNOW
**THE ONE WHO HOLDS
THE FUTURE!**

Proverbs 4

HEART GUARD

"I just need to go make my own mistakes!"

Maybe you've heard someone say that, or you've said it yourself. Since God has wired us to learn by experience, we may buy into this lie that the best way for us to learn is by failing. Don't get me wrong—failure is a great teacher, but when, in the name of learning, we choose sin despite warnings, it's self-sabotage.

Almost everything you know today you learned from the instruction and example of others. Think about the rise of DIY websites and TV shows. They're normally developed and published by people who have mastered a craft, excel in their field, or have achieved success at a hobby or task. Ultimately, it comes down to leadership. I learned to repair a toilet and change out a ceiling fan, but not by myself (thanks, YouTube). We learn best from one another.

As I mentioned earlier, Proverbs 1-9 were written from the viewpoint of a father speaking to his son. It's a bunch of fatherly wisdom being passed on to the next generation. Whichever stage of life you are currently in, you have a sphere of influence that will continue to grow as you grow. So many things in life can become teachable moments for you to pass on to others.

Solomon, speaking to his son, tells him…

> "LET YOUR HEART HOLD FAST MY WORDS;
> KEEP MY COMMANDMENTS, AND LIVE."
> — PROVERBS 4:4 —

In Proverbs 4, Solomon gives warnings and exhortation to the upcoming generation, telling which things to do (get wisdom and insight—verse 7) and which things to avoid (the path of the wicked and the way of the evil—verse 14). Much of his advice goes back to the main subject of Proverbs—an ongoing, consistent pursuit of wisdom and insight.

I'm thankful for the warnings, too. Any way I can avoid "the bread of wickedness" and "wine of violence," (verse 17) I will do that. Personally, I much prefer the bread of blessing and the wine of winners!

One of the most practical ways to follow the correct path and avoid the wrong path is found toward the end of the Proverb…

> "KEEP YOUR HEART WITH ALL VIGILANCE,
> FOR FROM IT FLOW THE SPRINGS OF LIFE."
> — PROVERBS 4:23 —

What we do flows out of who we are. What's in our heart is what will come out in our actions. Guarding our hearts will, in turn, guard our actions and inevitably our lifestyle. In other words, the way we spend our lives comes down to daily choices that stem from what we've allowed into our hearts. We are not the victims; we are the guardians.

Good news! There's no need to make your own mistakes; they've all been made already! So stay away and stay on task.

Dig Deeper

1. Which verse in Proverbs 4 stood out to you most and why?

_____

_____

_____

2. What are some mistakes you can avoid after learning from the example of others?

_____

_____

_____

3. What are some warnings you would give to others to help them avoid mistakes you've made?

_____

_____

_____

_____

"

THE WAY WE SPEND OUR LIVES
COMES DOWN TO DAILY CHOICES
THAT STEM FROM WHAT WE'VE
ALLOWED INTO OUR HEARTS. WE
ARE NOT THE VICTIMS; **WE ARE
THE GUARDIANS.**

Proverbs 5

HELL'S HONEY

Krispy Kreme, Cocoa Puffs, and Mountain Dew top today's lists of sweets, but in the pre-sugar overload days of the Bible, honey was every sweet tooth's desire. It's why God called the land He promised to Israel "a land flowing with milk and honey," and it's why the Psalmist says God's Word is sweeter than honey dripping from the comb (Psalm 19). When people in the Bible days thought of honey, their mouth started to water.

With that in mind, it's interesting that Solomon says that "the lips of a forbidden woman drip honey" (verse 3). In other words, she is enticing and seductive in the sweetest, most alluring ways possible.

One of the many valuable things about the Bible is its brutal honesty. The Bible never shies away from even the most controversial topics, including lust, immorality, and sex—inside and outside marriage.

Proverbs 5 begins a section of three Proverbs that speak to the topic of sexuality, purity, and the dangers of lust. As you will be able to tell, Solomon isn't shy about the wisdom he passes on to the next generation. He doesn't romanticize illicit encounters with a seductress or where this sin will lead. He says it straight without pulling any punches. And by the way, if anyone would know about the dangers of this sin, it was Solomon. In 2 Kings 3, the Bible says Solomon had 300 wives and 700 concubines. He had fallen for the lips of 1,000 forbidden women and the consequences were devastating.

Proverbs 5 isn't about suppressing our sexuality or making it out to be a negative, perverse thing. In fact, Solomon, like a good dad, makes sure his son is aware that sex within marriage is rewarding, beneficial, and intoxicating (verse 19). He draws his son's attention to the reality that marriage gives us a well to drink from to quench the thirst of our sexual nature.

> "DRINK WATER FROM YOUR OWN CISTERN,
> FLOWING WATER FROM YOUR OWN WELL."
> — PROVERBS 5:15 —

He goes on to say he should feel "blessed," he should "rejoice," he should be "filled with delight," and even goes as far as to say his son should "be intoxicated always" in his love for his wife. His argument is simple: *why get drunk on the lust of a woman whose lust leads to death, when he could be drunk on the love of his wife whose love leads to joy?*

Dig Deeper

1. Which verse in Proverbs 5 stood out to you most and why?

_____

_____

_____

_____

_____

_____

2. Modern culture is in sexual overdrive. Whether you are single, dating, or married, list some practical ways for you to resist the temptation of the "honey" of sexual sin.

_____

_____

_____

_____

_____

_____

"

SEX WITHIN MARRIAGE IS
REWARDING, BENEFICIAL,
AND **INTOXICATING.**

Proverbs 6

LEAN IN AND LISTEN

Have you ever been sitting in a coffee shop with a friend, trying to have a conversation without other people overhearing you? Or maybe you're the one listening in on someone else. I don't have to tell you about eavesdropping. You know all about it. You're smiling and nodding at the person you're sitting across the table from but your ears are tuned in to someone else's conversation. They're sharing juicy details about their awkward first date or talking about that scandal you read in the news yesterday. Sometimes it's hard not to listen in.

Proverbs 6 is like someone gave you permission to eavesdrop. We get to listen in on a heart-to-heart talk from a father to his son, sharing lots of important details and practical thoughts about life. There's a wide range of topics from personal finances, work ethic, the importance of being trustworthy, a list of things God hates, and even some in-your-face warnings about lust and adultery.

Very rarely will you walk away from eavesdropping and be well-equipped and wiser for doing so, but this is one of those rare cases. Here are a few takeaways from this valuable conversation…

Debt is simultaneously fueling the American dream and killing the dreamers. The first five verses of Proverbs 6 is a stern warning about the importance of getting out of debt and staying out. Living in debt is like being hunted (verse 5). If you've ever been hounded by creditors and collection agencies, you know that's all too true.

Mother nature has millions of awe-inspiring animals, enough that BBC and Disney will never be able to cover all of them in documentaries. An animal that is often overlooked by the National Geographic Channel gets its own time to shine in the pages of Scripture.

> "GO TO THE ANT, O SLUGGARD;
> CONSIDER HER WAYS, AND BE WISE."
> — PROVERBS 6:6 —

He goes on to explain the wisdom and work ethic of the ant, then derides the lazy, slumbering fool who can't get himself out of bed.

Laziness isn't the only thing this earthly father and our Heavenly Father despise, as he goes on to discuss the dangers of lying and lust as well.

Proverbs 5 warned of the tempting honey of the seductress, but Proverbs 6 warns of her smooth tongue and seductive, batting eyelashes. He warns that playing with lust is like playing with fire. There will be long-lasting, disfiguring, scarring burns.

> "HE WHO COMMITS ADULTERY LACKS SENSE;
> HE WHO DOES IT DESTROYS HIMSELF."
> — PROVERBS 6:32 —

Like any sin, the pleasure of lust is quickly fleeting. *Count the cost, then avoid at all costs.*

God's Word gives us clear instruction and warnings of the dangers that lie ahead. Thankfully, God allows us to listen in on these valuable conversations.

Dig Deeper

1. Which verse in Proverbs 6 stood out to you most and why?

_____

_____

_____

2. Laziness, lying, lust…what is a weakness of yours and what is something you can do today to fight it?

_____

_____

_____

3. If you continue in the sin you know you should abandon, what will it cost you? Is the long-lasting price worth the short-term pleasure you may be experiencing now?

_____

_____

_____

_____

"

PLAYING WITH LUST IS LIKE
PLAYING WITH FIRE. THERE WILL BE
LONG-LASTING, DISFIGURING,
SCARRING BURNS.

Proverbs 7

ESCALATOR TO HELL

I'm sure you've heard the song "Stairway to Heaven" by Led Zeppelin, but I'll bet you haven't heard of the "Escalator to Hell." It's a silky smooth ride to a place you never want to go and it happens in the most pleasurable way possible: lust.

When you were growing up, I imagine you learned the hard way that if your parents repeated themselves, you had better listen up. Proverbs 7 is the third chapter in a row that has warned us of the dangers of lust and sexual immorality. I'd say we had better pay attention!

Lust is a powerful temptation that has overtaken some of the strongest men and women throughout history: Samson, David, Mary Magdalene, as well as a saddening array of our contemporaries whose names fill our news feeds, some who were once household names, now for a different reason. Thankfully, God's Word contains the wisdom you need that will "keep you from the forbidden woman" (verse 5) or whatever your sin of the day may be.

The world will tell you to follow your heart, but Proverbs 7 is a sad tale of what happens when you do that. It tells the story of a young man who ignorantly and selfishly followed his heart, falling into the seductive trap of adultery.

All temptation—lust, greed, pride, etc.—is slippery and seductive. Just as a fish doesn't bite a hook without a worm, sin's sway is only successful because it is seductive. Hebrews 11 mentions the passing pleasures of sin, stating a fact we all know to be true: sin is fun—for a season. The young man in Proverbs 7 had a good time—at first. He met the seductress under the cover of darkness and as she kissed him, she lured him in with fancy bedding, expensive perfumes, and promises of a night filled with pleasure. But, notice the contrast as he descends into her abyss…

"WITH MUCH SEDUCTIVE SPEECH
SHE PERSUADES HIM;
WITH HER SMOOTH TALK SHE COMPELS HIM.
ALL AT ONCE HE FOLLOWS HER,
AS AN OX GOES TO THE SLAUGHTER…"
— PROVERBS 7:21-22 —

From the outside looking in, we are told where the seduction is leading. The chapter ends with this dark warning…

"HER HOUSE IS THE WAY TO SHEOL,
GOING DOWN TO THE CHAMBERS OF DEATH."
— PROVERBS 7:27 —

It's the escalator to hell. It's smooth, requires no real effort beyond getting on board, and once you're on, you just enjoy the ride as the momentum carries you lower and lower.

We are told that the young man in the story "does not know that it will cost him his life" (verse 23); *but we do!* Consider yourself warned. To continue on in sin would be like punching the gas when the road sign reads "bridge out ahead."

Dig Deeper

1. Which verse in Proverbs 7 stood out to you most and why?

_____

_____

_____

2. Staying out of temptation begins by naming your temptation. What is one of the biggest areas of weakness for you (lust, greed, envy, pride, etc.)?

_____

_____

_____

3. Now that you've named an area of weakness, what are three ways you can immediately begin guarding yourself against that temptation?

_____

_____

_____

_____

"

SIN'S SWAY IS ONLY
SUCCESSFUL **BECAUSE**
IT IS SEDUCTIVE.

Proverbs 8

THE BEST OF THE BEST

We've all hung out with people who seem to like themselves a little too much. They're constantly talking about their achievements, accolades, abilities, and awards. Hanging around someone like that can be exhausting. But what if all the bragging is correct? What if it's less bragging and more stating facts? That's the case with Proverbs 8.

If the subject of Proverbs 8 was anything or anyone besides wisdom itself, it would be a chapter full of bragging. Since it's all about wisdom, it's simply a list of facts—some pretty amazing facts, actually!

Proverbs 8 personifies wisdom and lists some amazing things about it...

> "HEAR, FOR I WILL SPEAK *NOBLE* THINGS,
> AND FROM MY LIPS WILL COME WHAT IS
> *RIGHT*, FOR MY MOUTH WILL UTTER *TRUTH*;
> WICKEDNESS IS AN ABOMINATION TO MY
> LIPS. ALL THE WORDS OF MY MOUTH ARE
> *RIGHTEOUS*; THERE IS NOTHING TWISTED
> OR CROOKED IN THEM. THEY ARE ALL
> *STRAIGHT* TO HIM WHO UNDERSTANDS, AND
> *RIGHT* TO THOSE WHO FIND KNOWLEDGE."
> — PROVERBS 8:6-8 —

Just look at that list of adjectives! Noble, right, truth, righteous, straight... Those are some strong attributes. No wonder we are told to go after wisdom instead of silver, gold, or jewels. After all, wisdom is what we need to do the things God has called us to do.

Think about the desperate lengths people go to in order to figure out what to do. King Saul went undercover and had a fortune teller call up the spirit of Samuel from the dead. Samuel's appearance even scared the seer! The prophets of Baal cut themselves, danced, and screamed for half of a day on top of Mt. Carmel, but nothing happened. In our day even, people turn to astrology, crystal balls, ouija boards, and even social media to figure out what to do. The answer is much simpler than that, however.

> "BY ME (WISDOM) KINGS REIGN, AND RULERS DECREE WHAT IS JUST; BY ME PRINCES RULE, AND NOBLES, ALL WHO GOVERN JUSTLY."
> — PROVERBS 8:15-16 —

No wonder God was so pleased when He gave King Solomon the opportunity to ask for anything he wanted. When most of us would have wished for more wishes (everyone knows that's what you do if a genie appears!), Solomon asked for wisdom. God gladly answered that prayer because as James 1:5 reminds us, if we lack wisdom, we should ask God and He'll give it liberally and without reproach! *Many of us don't have the wisdom we need to do what we are called to simply because we haven't taken the time to ask and listen.*

The wisest thing anyone can do is put their faith in Jesus. Although the context of Proverbs 8 is wisdom, it ends prophetically and poetically pointing to Jesus…

> "FOR WHOEVER FINDS ME FINDS LIFE AND OBTAINS FAVOR FROM THE LORD, BUT HE WHO FAILS TO FIND ME INJURES HIMSELF; ALL WHO HATE ME LOVE DEATH."
> — PROVERBS 8:35-36 —

Dig Deeper

1. Which verse in Proverbs 8 stood out to you most and why?

_____

_____

_____

_____

_____

2. Take a minute to write out a prayer to God asking for wisdom, then pray it. Ask God for the wisdom you need to raise your kids, discern His voice, navigate a relationship, etc., then keep praying that prayer regularly.

_____

_____

_____

_____

"

MANY OF US DON'T HAVE THE
WISDOM WE NEED TO DO WHAT WE
ARE CALLED TO SIMPLY BECAUSE
WE HAVEN'T TAKEN THE TIME
TO **ASK AND LISTEN.**

Proverbs 9

ARCH NEMESIS

So far, most of Proverbs has been about the main character: wisdom. Proverbs 9 introduces us to wisdom's arch nemesis: folly. As they're contrasted against each other, the differences become very apparent.

Wisdom is a hard worker. I immediately want to hang out with wisdom because the first thing she's seen doing is making a feast—meat, wine, and elaborate table settings. But what is a feast without some guests? As the feast is prepared, she begins to invite people to join her…

> "WHOEVER IS SIMPLE, LET HIM TURN IN HERE!
> TO HIM WHO LACKS SENSE SHE SAYS, 'COME,
> EAT OF MY BREAD AND DRINK OF THE WINE I
> HAVE MIXED. LEAVE YOUR SIMPLE WAYS, AND
> LIVE, AND WALK IN THE WAY OF INSIGHT.'"
> — PROVERBS 9:4-6 —

Wisdom is constantly making room for those who want to live to the fullest.

Folly is also inviting guests in and although her invitation sounds identical to that of wisdom, the end result of befriending folly is much different…

> "'WHOEVER IS SIMPLE, LET HIM TURN IN
> HERE!' AND TO HIM WHO LACKS SENSE SHE
> SAYS, 'STOLEN WATER IS SWEET, AND BREAD
> EATEN IN SECRET IS PLEASANT.' BUT HE DOES
> NOT KNOW THAT THE DEAD ARE THERE, THAT
> HER GUESTS ARE IN THE DEPTHS OF SHEOL."
> — PROVERBS 9:16-18 —

The invitation started out identical, but the end results couldn't be more opposite: *life and death*.

Proverbs 9 is a crystal clear reminder of the outcomes of the lifestyle we choose. Wisdom requires hard work and diligence but leads to life; whereas folly is lazy, loud, seductive, ignorant, and it leads to death.

Toward the middle of the Proverb, we learn a valuable and seemingly counterintuitive insight about wisdom...

> "DO NOT REPROVE A SCOFFER, OR
> HE WILL HATE YOU; REPROVE A WISE
> MAN, AND HE WILL LOVE YOU."
> — PROVERBS 9:8 —

The longer we give into the invitations and temptations of foolishness, the less we want to listen to the advice and counsel of those around us. It's a downward spiral: foolishness leads to less listening, and when listening decreases, foolishness increases.

However, if we desire wisdom, we will listen. We will pay attention when others speak into our lives. Our lives begin an upward ascent: listening to wise counsel leads to more wisdom, which creates a desire to listen to more wisdom...

Which will define your life - wisdom or folly?

Dig Deeper

1. Which verse in Proverbs 9 stood out to you most and why?

_____

_____

_____

2. What are some of the main contributing factors of the foolish decisions you have made or foolish actions you have taken?

_____

_____

_____

3. What are some practical ways to avoid the temptation to make those decisions in the future?

_____

_____

_____

_____

"

IF WE DESIRE WISDOM,
WE WILL LISTEN. WE WILL PAY
ATTENTION WHEN OTHERS SPEAK
INTO OUR LIVES, **CAUSING OUR
LIVES TO BEGIN AN**
UPWARD ASCENT.

Proverbs 10

COMPARE AND CONTRAST

Have you ever ordered the big, juicy cheeseburger you saw pictured on the menu, then were severely disappointed when your meal arrived? When you compare the picture with the real burger, it looks much different. "I ordered that, but I got this." It's a big contrast.

Speaking of contrast, Proverbs 10 begins a new style of wisdom poetry where Solomon contrasts wisdom and foolishness. Proverbs 10 is actually where the real "proverbs" begin. Proverbs 1-9 were proverbial in their content, but now begins the compare and contrast style that typifies most of the rest of the book. For most of the rest of Proverbs, in the first half of each verse, Solomon shows a picture of the ideal situation (wisdom), then contrasts that with the reality of the outcome of foolishness in the second half of the verse.

You'll find the word "but" many times throughout the rest of the book; twenty-five times in just this chapter! There's a constant contrast between wisdom and foolishness on a variety of topics: a wise son and a foolish son, the righteous and the wicked, integrity and crookedness, those who listen to instruction and those who reject correction, and so on. Here are a few of my favorites from chapter 10...

> "THE LORD DOES NOT LET THE RIGHTEOUS
> GO HUNGRY, BUT HE THWARTS THE
> CRAVING OF THE WICKED."
> — PROVERBS 10:3 —

We aren't considered "righteous" because we've done a lot of righteous works, but because Jesus is righteous and in Him we are counted as righteous. God promises to take care of His kids. The wicked, on the other hand, are on their own. When we reject God as the Provider, providing for ourselves is on us. I don't know about you, but I'd rather God provide for me than for that weight to be on my shoulders.

> "HE WHO GATHERS IN SUMMER IS A
> PRUDENT SON, BUT HE WHO SLEEPS IN
> HARVEST IS A SON WHO BRINGS SHAME."
> — PROVERBS 10:5 —

I used to be the sleeping son listed in verse 5. Just ask my dad. I would sleep until 1:00 pm on Saturdays if I could and I could not figure out why my dad was up so early. As an adult, I've now learned that time is a valuable non-renewable resource that I cannot afford to throw away. I have to be diligent with my time. Lazy people not only miss out on the harvest but bring shame on themselves.

> "WHOEVER WALKS IN INTEGRITY WALKS
> SECURELY, BUT HE WHO MAKES HIS WAYS
> CROOKED WILL BE FOUND OUT."
> — PROVERBS 10:9 —

My teenage years were proof that our sin will find us out. You may fool every other person around you, but you can never fool God. He sees all and knows all, and as long as you are one of His kids, He'll only let you run for so long. Honesty and openness lead to a life of integrity, which brings great security.

Here's one more of my favorites…

> "LIKE VINEGAR TO THE TEETH AND SMOKE
> TO THE EYES, SO IS THE SLUGGARD
> TO THOSE WHO SEND HIM."
> — PROVERBS 10:26 —

Don't be the sluggard of verse 26 that makes everyone's lives more painful. At all costs, I want to avoid living in a way that causes people to describe me as "vinegar on their teeth" or "smoke in their eyes."

Dig Deeper

1. Which verse in Proverbs 10 stood out to you most and why?

_____

_____

_____

_____

_____

2. Vinegar on the teeth and smoke in the eyes are painful and leave a bad taste in your mouth. What are some practical ways we can make sure we leave people with a good taste?

_____

_____

_____

_____

_____

"

WE AREN'T CONSIDERED
"RIGHTEOUS" BECAUSE WE'VE DONE
A LOT OF RIGHTEOUS WORKS BUT
BECAUSE JESUS IS RIGHTEOUS AND **IN
HIM, WE ARE COUNTED AS**
RIGHTEOUS.

Proverbs 11

THE STRUGGLE IS REAL

The struggle between good and evil is everywhere we look. It's the plot of every movie, the structure of every novel, and the reality of our daily lives. "Get the waffle fries and a regular lemonade," the devil on one shoulder says as I stand in line at Chick-Fil-A. "You really should go with the side salad and diet lemonade," the angel on my other shoulder reminds me. You know what I'm talking about. The struggle is real.

That age-old struggle is so much deeper than maintaining a healthy diet; it's about maintaining a healthy soul. Thankfully, we have Solomon's wisdom to keep us strong in the struggle. Here are some timely reminders...

> "RICHES DO NOT PROFIT IN THE DAY
> OF WRATH, BUT RIGHTEOUSNESS
> DELIVERS FROM DEATH."
> — PROVERBS 11:4 —

The ancient Egyptians filled tombs and coffins with gold, gems, and millions of dollars of valuables, thinking that the mummified corpse would take the riches with them into the afterlife. Even today, I've been to funerals where people stuff money and possessions into the casket before it is closed. But Job nailed it when he said, "Naked I came from my mother's womb, and naked I shall return" (Job 1:21). We brought nothing into this world and we can take nothing with us. Wisdom and righteous living are better than gold because they last.

> "WHOEVER IS STEADFAST IN RIGHTEOUSNESS
> WILL LIVE, BUT HE WHO PURSUES EVIL WILL DIE."
> — PROVERBS 11:19 —

Doing the right thing can be pretty easy when you're surrounded by people who encourage it, but what about when you're not? What about when you're the only one fighting for truth? That's what Solomon means by being "steadfast in righteousness." It means being unwilling to compromise or bend to popular opinion. The good news is that life is promised to those who remain steadfast, not because they were steadfast, but because *their steadfastness was proof of their righteousness.*

> "WHOEVER TRUSTS IN HIS RICHES
> WILL FALL, BUT THE RIGHTEOUS WILL
> FLOURISH LIKE A GREEN LEAF."
> — PROVERBS 11:28 —

As verse 4 reminded us, riches can't be trusted. You can bank *with* Benjamins but don't bank *on* them. Money is a shaky foundation. In contrast, however, is the righteous that flourishes like a green leaf. Green leaves are evidence of a well-working root system. The roots not only keep the plant in place, but they funnel nutrients to the plant, stem, and leaves. The flourishing lives of the righteous will be visible on the outside due to health on the inside.

Dig Deeper

1. Which verse in Proverbs 11 stood out to you most and why?

_____

_____

_____

_____

_____

_____

2. What is an area of "wickedness" in your life that you can work with God to eliminate from your life?

_____

_____

_____

_____

_____

_____

"

LIFE IS PROMISED TO THOSE
WHO REMAIN STEADFAST, NOT
BECAUSE THEY WERE STEADFAST,
**BUT BECAUSE THEIR STEADFASTNESS
WAS PROOF OF THEIR**
RIGHTEOUSNESS.

Proverbs 12

DOUBLE DISCIPLINE

When you think of discipline, a couple of things may come to your mind:

Maybe it's the spanking spoon (or belt) that was used on you as a kid. Your parents used it to *discipline* you when you broke the rules.

Or maybe you think of discipline in the context of training. We discipline ourselves (some more than others) to accomplish goals and tasks. It takes self-discipline to go to the gym, choose steamed broccoli over french fries, and live a well-balanced life.

Both of these types of discipline are mentioned in Proverbs 12 and in certain ways, both types of discipline involve pain. We tend to dodge pain at all costs, but it's important to realize that pain can be a good thing.

Here are a few things Proverbs 12 teaches us about discipline...

> "WHOEVER LOVES DISCIPLINE
> LOVES KNOWLEDGE, BUT HE WHO
> HATES REPROOF IS STUPID."
> — PROVERBS 12:1 —

"Loves discipline"—now there's a unique phrase. "Love" and "discipline" don't normally go together unless you come to a clear understanding of the goal of discipline. Discipline is our training ground. The author of Hebrews reminds us that when God disciplines us, He's simply treating us as His kids (Hebrews 12:7). He goes on to say, "For the moment all discipline seems painful rather than pleasant, but later it yields the peaceful fruit of righteousness to those who have been trained by it" (Hebrews 12:11).

The product of discipline is worth the pain of discipline.

One of the areas that we need the most self-discipline with is our words.

> **"THERE IS ONE WHOSE RASH WORDS ARE**
> **LIKE SWORD THRUSTS, BUT THE TONGUE**
> **OF THE WISE BRINGS HEALING."**
> **— PROVERBS 12:18 —**

Speaking of pain, if we don't discipline ourselves, our words will eventually cause pain (like sword thrusts) in the lives of the people around us. It takes self-discipline to have a tongue that brings healing.

Discipline is also required when it comes to growth and obedience...

> **"NO ONE IS ESTABLISHED BY WICKEDNESS, BUT THE**
> **ROOT OF THE RIGHTEOUS WILL NEVER BE MOVED."**
> **— PROVERBS 12:3 —**

> **"WHOEVER IS WICKED COVETS THE**
> **SPOIL OF EVILDOERS, BUT THE ROOT**
> **OF THE RIGHTEOUS BEARS FRUIT."**
> **— PROVERBS 12:12 —**

We talked about roots in Proverbs 11, but the theme appears again here. Just like when you were growing up, if your mom repeated herself, you better pay extra attention. The same principle applies here. It's repeated so it's easily remembered.

Solomon reminds us here that the root of the righteous (those whose faith is in Jesus for salvation) will never be moved. In other words, while storms rage around us, we are steadfast and immovable because we have a firm foundation where we grow and are grounded in God. Verse 12 follows up with the reminder that not only do our righteous roots keep us firm, they also make us fruitful.

A fruit-filled, firmly-rooted life will require a humble response to painful discipline and a faith-filled pursuit of self-discipline.

Dig Deeper

1. Which verse in Proverbs 12 stood out to you most and why?

_____

_____

_____

2. What needs to change in your life in order to help you respond better to God's discipline?

_____

_____

_____

3. Are you guilty of speaking to others in a way that feels like you're thrusting them with a sword? Ouch. What are two things you can do to begin changing that? Make it your goal to use your words to build others up, not to scare them or scar them.

_____

_____

_____

"

A FRUIT -FILLED, FIRMLY-ROOTED
LIFE WILL REQUIRE A HUMBLE
RESPONSE TO A PAINFUL DISCIPLINE
AND A **FAITH-FILLED PURSUIT OF
SELF-DISCIPLINE**.

Proverbs 13

GODLY GUARDRAILS

I've never seen so many guardrails bent, twisted, or completely missing as I have since we moved to Tennessee. I'm not sure what's going on with the Southern drivers but the guardrails seem to be a magnet for cars. Guardrails aren't meant to be a ramp for us to launch off of; they're designed to be a guard for us to bump off of, realigning us to where we need to be.

Proverbs is filled with helpful guardrails, getting us back in our lane and safely to our destination.

> "WHOEVER GUARDS HIS MOUTH
> PRESERVES HIS LIFE; HE WHO OPENS
> WIDE HIS LIPS COMES TO RUIN."
> — PROVERBS 13:3 —

"Sticks and stones may break my bones, but words can never hurt me." That's cute, but so far from the truth. We've all been hurt by words from others and we've all hurt others with our words. Solomon says we preserve our lives by guarding our mouths, but what does that look like, practically speaking? Guarding our mouths means thinking before we speak, being gentle with our words, and speaking the truth in love. Just because it's true doesn't mean it should be said, but when hard truth does need to be said, we should say it gently.

> "WHOEVER DESPISES THE WORD BRINGS
> DESTRUCTION ON HIMSELF, BUT HE WHO REVERES
> THE COMMANDMENT WILL BE REWARDED."
> — PROVERBS 13:13 —

"Revering the commandment" means following the rules. God's Word is full of guidelines and guardrails that are put in place for our protection. Like a loving parent tells their children not to run with scissors or play in the street, God puts rules in place for sex, finances, relationships, and more. Following those commandments will result in rewards like confidence and a clean conscience.

> "WHOEVER WALKS WITH THE WISE
> BECOMES WISE, BUT THE COMPANION
> OF FOOLS WILL SUFFER HARM."
> — PROVERBS 13:20 —

Godly friends can function as guardrails but ungodly friends can be hazardous. "Walking with the wise" has the idea of being in sync with their values, lifestyle, and destination. Every fool needs a wise friend to help them get to where they need to be, but always pay attention to who is doing the influencing in a relationship.

> "WHOEVER SPARES THE ROD HATES
> HIS SON, BUT HE WHO LOVES HIM IS
> DILIGENT TO DISCIPLINE HIM."
> — PROVERBS 13:24 —

Although our culture has decided physical discipline is not good for children, the Bible—especially Proverbs—has a different opinion. That's a pretty bold statement that we hate our children if we don't discipline them, but it makes sense. An undisciplined child is like a dangerous, windy road with no guardrails or warning signs. Every kid needs correction, guidance, and realignment; so parents, be diligent (and gracious) in your discipline. After all, because God loves us, He disciplines us (see Hebrews 12).

Dig Deeper

1. Which verse in Proverbs 13 stood out to you most and why?

_____

_____

_____

_____

_____

_____

2. Which of the guardrails mentioned do you struggle the most with and what are some ways you can follow it better?

_____

_____

_____

_____

_____

_____

"

JUST BECAUSE IT'S TRUE DOESN'T
MEAN IT SHOULD BE SAID, BUT
WHEN HARD TRUTH DOES
NEED TO BE SAID, **WE SHOULD
SAY IT GENTLY.**

Proverbs 14

EYES ON THE PRIZE

"If you smile for our family pictures, I have a bag of M&M's waiting in the car for you!" Some people may call that "bribery" but I prefer the more positive term, "motivation." My wife and I try not to resort to this sort of motivation very often but sometimes, especially with a family photo shoot, some additional motivation is required.

Even Jesus benefited from motivation. Hebrews 12:2 says Jesus endured the cross "because of the joy that was set before Him." The promise of victory and joy that would come after the cross enabled Jesus to endure the excruciating physical and spiritual pain of the cross!

We get in trouble when we are only focused on the here and now. Although we should be present in the moment, it's wise to keep our eyes on the prize ahead. Proverbs 14 provides some wisdom along those lines.

> "THERE IS A WAY THAT SEEMS
> RIGHT TO A MAN, BUT ITS END
> IS THE WAY TO DEATH."
> — PROVERBS 14:12 —

Sometimes what "seems" right is far from it. If something can feel right but lead to death, we need to be very careful where we are allowing life to lead us. But if it seems right, how can we know if we're being led astray? Simple: God won't lead you in the way of death. If you are reading His Word, speaking to Him in prayer, and following the wise counsel of Godly friends, you can rest assured the path you're following won't lead to death, even if it feels like death while you're traveling.

> "THE BACKSLIDER IN HEART WILL BE
> FILLED WITH THE FRUIT OF HIS WAYS,
> AND A GOOD MAN WILL BE FILLED
> WITH THE FRUIT OF HIS WAYS."
> — PROVERBS 14:14 —

This verse could be simplified as "you reap what you sow." You don't plant watermelon seeds and expect to grow an orange tree. Similarly, you should know that the thoughts, actions, and habits you are planting in your life and relationships will produce fruit. But is it the type of fruit you want in your life? Taking your eyes off of the prize and living for the thrill of the moment will not lead you where you want to go. Be cautious.

> "IN THE FEAR OF THE LORD ONE HAS STRONG
> CONFIDENCE, AND HIS CHILDREN WILL
> HAVE A REFUGE. THE FEAR OF THE LORD IS
> A FOUNTAIN OF LIFE, THAT ONE MAY TURN
> AWAY FROM THE SNARES OF DEATH."
> — PROVERBS 14:26–27 —

The fear of the Lord isn't so much about fear as it is about reverence and awe. When we have a healthy fear of God, we have confidence knowing He is in control even when life feels out of control. That confidence leads to Godly protection and confidence for those around us as well! Not only will fearing God produce confidence, but it's a fountain of life! It keeps us away from temptation and distraction, with our eyes and lives focused on eternity.

Dig Deeper

1. Which verse in Proverbs 14 stood out to you most and why?

_____

_____

_____

2. In which areas of your life have you taken your eyes off of the prize? Relationships? God's Word? Parenting? Your job?

_____

_____

_____

_____

3. How can you realign your focus on eternity in those problematic areas?

_____

_____

_____

_____

"

TAKING YOUR EYES OFF OF
THE PRIZE AND LIVING FOR THE THRILL
OF THE MOMENT WILL NOT
LEAD YOU WHERE YOU WANT
TO GO . **BE CAUTIOUS.**

$\mathfrak{Proverbs}$ 15

MR. KNOW-IT-ALL

Most kids grow up with the healthy fear that their parents must have eyes in the back of their heads. Once when I was wearing a hat, my kids thought they could get away with something since it must be covering up my extra set of eyes. Wrong! I see all and know all...or at least I want them to think I do!

Our Heavenly Father really does see all and know all. Just listen to Proverbs 15...

> "THE EYES OF THE LORD ARE IN
> EVERY PLACE, KEEPING WATCH ON
> THE EVIL AND THE GOOD."
> — PROVERBS 15:3 —

Because God is watching everything and is in the know about all details of life, that puts new meaning behind everything we do, say, and think. *Since God sees everything, everything matters.*

> "THE HEART OF HIM WHO HAS
> UNDERSTANDING SEEKS KNOWLEDGE, BUT
> THE MOUTHS OF FOOLS FEED ON FOLLY."
> — PROVERBS 15:14 —

Since God sees everything, what we are taking into our minds and hearts matters. Verse 14 reminds us that we can waste our time feeding on folly or invest our time wisely by seeking knowledge. The latter is the obvious wise choice. *Since "you are what you eat," then what you spend your time consuming is what you will become.*

> "A HOT-TEMPERED MAN STIRS UP
> STRIFE, BUT HE WHO IS SLOW TO
> ANGER QUIETS CONTENTION."
> — PROVERBS 15:18 —

Since God sees and knows all, how we treat others matters. We have all lost our tempers, raised our voices, and said things we regret in the heat of the moment. We should aim to be described as people who are "slow to anger." In other words, it should take a lot to get under our skin. Paul, in the New Testament book of Galatians, calls this "longsuffering." When we know God sees our circumstances, we know He can empower us with longsuffering—the ability to suffer long, even when we want to be upset and let everyone know about it!

> "WITHOUT COUNSEL PLANS FAIL, BUT
> WITH MANY ADVISERS THEY SUCCEED."
> — PROVERBS 15:22 —

Since God sees everything, He will lead us in the way we should go. In addition to His Word, His Spirit, and the desires He has placed in us, one of the primary ways He leads us is through the Godly counsel of the people He has placed around us. As you seek to make decisions in life, make sure you are well-informed. Talk to God first and throughout the process, but make sure to listen to "many advisers" who are also listening to God.

> "THE PATH OF LIFE LEADS UPWARD
> FOR THE PRUDENT, THAT HE MAY TURN
> AWAY FROM SHEOL BENEATH."
> — PROVERBS 15:24 —

When we forget that God cares about the details of our lives and we choose to live for ourselves, life will quickly turn into a downward spiral. However, "for the prudent" (or the wise person), life is an upward spiral! Since God sees everything, He is the only One worth following. He knows where He's going and can be trusted every step of the way.

1. Which verse in Proverbs 15 stood out to you most and why?

    _____

    _____

    _____

    _____

    _____

    _____

2. How should God's omniscience (His knowledge of every detail of life—past, present, and future) impact how we live our lives?

    _____

    _____

    _____

    _____

    _____

    _____

"

SINCE "YOU ARE WHAT YOU
EAT," THEN WHAT YOU SPEND
YOUR TIME CONSUMING IS
WHAT YOU WILL BECOME.

Proverbs 16

DON'T MARRY YOUR PLANS

Marriage is meant to be a lifelong covenant, unbroken by even the most challenging circumstances. That's how marriage should be, but sometimes we mistakenly approach our own plans, timelines, and agendas with that same commitment. Then when they fall apart, we're distraught and confused.

Make plans, but don't marry them.

Planning is wise, but hold your plans with an open hand as you trust God to steer the course of your life. Here's how Solomon put it...

> **"COMMIT YOUR WORK TO THE LORD, AND**
> **YOUR PLANS WILL BE ESTABLISHED."**
> **— PROVERBS 16:3 —**

Committing your work to the Lord means doing whatever you're doing to honor Him. Could you go to that school/marry that person/do that on the weekend/take that promotion as a way of honoring Jesus?

Yes? Do it!

No? Don't waste your time.

> **"THE HEART OF MAN PLANS HIS WAY, BUT**
> **THE LORD ESTABLISHES HIS STEPS."**
> **— PROVERBS 16:9 —**

Verse 3 and verse 9 go hand in hand, reminding us of the importance of planning, but allowing God to lead the way. As we continue through

Proverbs, you'll read more and more about the importance of planning, strategizing, and preparing for the future, but there's a danger in becoming too attached to our plans. Avoid the temptation to make plans and ask God to bless them. Instead, get in the habit of being led by God in your planning. He promises to establish (make firm and sure) your steps.

> **"PRIDE GOES BEFORE DESTRUCTION, AND**
> **A HAUGHTY SPIRIT BEFORE A FALL."**
> **— PROVERBS 16:18 —**

Pride leads us to the false notion that our plans, our timeline, and our desires are the best. Pride gives us tunnel vision with our way of doing things. Solomon warns us here of the devastating consequences of pride: it will inevitably lead to a fall. We all know that is not what we are aiming for! We avoid the fall by avoiding pride and we avoid pride by cultivating a spirit of humility. And by the way, *humility isn't thinking less of yourself* ("I'm no good… I'm not gifted… I'm not that great…"), *humility is thinking of yourself less.*

> **"WHOEVER GIVES THOUGHT TO THE WORD**
> **WILL DISCOVER GOOD, AND BLESSED**
> **IS HE WHO TRUSTS IN THE LORD."**
> **— PROVERBS 16:20 —**

LIVE BY THIS VERSE! If you will live by this, you'll never go wrong. In fact, any time you look back on your life and see that you've gone astray, I guarantee you can analyze the situation and realize you did not "give thought to the word" and/or "trust in the Lord."

> **"THE LOT IS CAST INTO THE LAP, BUT ITS**
> **EVERY DECISION IS FROM THE LORD."**
> **— PROVERBS 16:33 —**

Some of God's favorite pseudonyms to work under are "coincidence" and "it just so happened." God is intricately involved in the details of our lives and constantly weaving them together to point us closer to Him. Trust Him, even when life feels "random."

Dig Deeper

1. Which verse in Proverbs 16 stood out to you most and why?

_____

_____

_____

2. What are some plans, timelines, and/or relationships in your life you need to surrender and commit to the Lord?

_____

_____

_____

3. What are some specific things you can do to let go and let God take control of them?

_____

_____

_____

_____

"
HUMILITY ISN'T THINKING
LESS OF YOURSELF; **IT IS THINKING
OF YOURSELF LESS.**

Proverbs 17

BETTER TOGETHER

Solitaire. Single scoop ice cream. A one man show. What do all of these things have in common? They're all on their own. Being on your own is fine in those cases, but we were not meant to live life on our own. In fact, in another of Solomon's wisdom books, Ecclesiastes, he says, "Two are better than one, because they have a good reward for their toil" (Ecclesiastes 4:9).

After all, what's the peanut butter without the jelly or the salt without the pepper?

Proverbs 17 gives some practical wisdom on how we relate to one another...

> "WHOEVER COVERS AN OFFENSE SEEKS
> LOVE, BUT HE WHO REPEATS A MATTER
> SEPARATES CLOSE FRIENDS."
> — PROVERBS 17:9 —

Covering an offense doesn't mean denying the truth or scandalously covering for someone so they don't get caught. Covering an offense means not broadcasting their failure. Sin must be dealt with but in the most loving, gracious manner possible, seeking to protect the person's integrity and reputation as much as possible. And be careful of spreading gossip under the guise of prayer requests on the person's behalf. Christians are especially good at "sanctified gossip!"

> "THE BEGINNING OF STRIFE IS LIKE
> LETTING OUT WATER, SO QUIT BEFORE
> THE QUARREL BREAKS OUT."
> — PROVERBS 17:14 —

When our church was just eight months old, we lost everything due to a flood that hit our city. Interestingly, it wasn't because it rained too much in Clarksville—it was because officials opened a dam in Nashville! Since we are downstream from Nashville, their decision to open the dam led to a devastating flood. It's similar with anger. When strife begins, it's just a small, manageable leak. We need to be quick to patch things up before the dam breaks and devastation occurs within the relationship.

> **"A FRIEND LOVES AT ALL TIMES, AND A BROTHER IS BORN FOR ADVERSITY."**
> **— PROVERBS 17:17 —**

Love is not an emotion; it's a choice. It's easy to love—and to feel the emotions that surround love—when things are running smooth. But, a true friend loves even when it's hard to love—even in adversity. Are you a friend who continues to love even when it's hard? Adversity is one of the most important times for us to choose love.

> **"WHOEVER RESTRAINS HIS WORDS HAS KNOWLEDGE, AND HE WHO HAS A COOL SPIRIT IS A MAN OF UNDERSTANDING."**
> **— PROVERBS 17:27 —**

Restraining our words is the patchwork on the dam we discussed earlier. When we choose to let our tongue loose, the dam breaks and devastation occurs. The antidote to a hot temper and fiery words is "a cool spirit." Restraining our words and keeping a cool spirit is like pouring water on a hot fire—it can extinguish the danger and prevent potential disaster. Managing our spirit and maintaining a cool spirit requires the work of the Holy Spirit. Galatians 5 says that part of the proof that the Holy Spirit is in you is self-control. Let the Spirit give you the strength to restrain your words and keep a cool spirit.

Dig Deeper

1. Which verse in Proverbs 17 stood out to you most and why?

_____

_____

_____

_____

_____

2. Are there some "dams" in danger of rupturing in your life right now? What is some patchwork you can immediately begin implementing that will help prevent further damage or future disaster?

_____

_____

_____

_____

_____

"

RESTRAINING OUR WORDS AND
KEEPING A COOL SPIRIT IS LIKE
POURING WATER ON A HOT FIRE - IT
CAN EXTINGUISH THE DANGER
AND PREVENT POTENTIAL
DISASTER.

Proverbs 18

FLEX THAT MUSCLE FOR GOOD

The tongue is a powerful muscle—group of muscles, that is. The tongue is comprised of eight interwoven muscles and are the only muscles in the body that work independently of the skeleton. Measuring from the epiglottis (the flap of cartilage in the mouth at the back of the tongue) to the tip, the average tongue is only about three inches long. Although it is comparatively small to the rest of the body, it is extremely powerful. In fact, the book of James compares the tongue to the bit that controls a horse and the rudder that steers a ship!

Proverbs talks a lot about the power of our words and it's a theme that runs throughout Proverbs 18.

> "WHOEVER ISOLATES HIMSELF SEEKS
> HIS OWN DESIRE; HE BREAKS OUT
> AGAINST ALL SOUND JUDGMENT."
> — PROVERBS 18:1 —

At first glance, this opening verse may not seem like it has much to do with speech, but you're wrong. This is a clear reminder of the importance of intentionally allowing Godly voices to speak into our lives.

I love the Bible's honesty here. There's no need to hold back. Solomon is simply saying that on our own, without Godly voices in our lives, we are selfish ("seeks his own desire") and stupid ("breaks out against all sound judgment"). Isolation never leads anyone anywhere good.

> ## "THE WORDS OF A MAN'S MOUTH
> ARE DEEP WATERS; THE FOUNTAIN OF
> WISDOM IS A BUBBLING BROOK."
> — PROVERBS 18:4 —

Words spoken to us and by us have deep, profound meaning. The words we allow to come out of our mouths and into our ears can have long-lasting, life-altering consequences, for good or bad. Thankfully, as Solomon reminds us, "the fountain of wisdom is a bubbling brook." Doesn't "bubbling brook" sound refreshing? When we fill our ears and hearts with wisdom, our words become a never-ending stream of refreshment to those around us!

> ## "THE ONE WHO STATES HIS CASE
> FIRST SEEMS RIGHT, UNTIL THE OTHER
> COMES AND EXAMINES HIM."
> — PROVERBS 18:17 —

We have all learned this the hard way. When we only hear one side of the argument, it's easy to demonize the other person. But, there's always a second side to the story, isn't there? Don't fall for this trap of immediately assuming the worst of someone based on only part of the story. Our goal should be to stand for truth while protecting, being gracious, and always thinking the best of others.

> ## "DEATH AND LIFE ARE IN THE POWER
> OF THE TONGUE, AND THOSE WHO
> LOVE IT WILL EAT ITS FRUITS."
> — PROVERBS 18:21 —

If you didn't get it yet, I don't know if it can be stated much clearer than this: That three-inch long combination of muscles is about so much more than tasting food. It holds the power of life and death! Use your words wisely and make sure your words are producing life-giving fruit.

Dig Deeper

1. Which verse in Proverbs 18 stood out to you most and why?

_____

_____

_____

_____

_____

_____

2. Think of some areas of your life where you are isolated. Since verse 1 warns of the dangerous of isolation, what can you begin doing to include others in those problematic areas of your life?

_____

_____

_____

_____

_____

"

WHEN WE FILL OUR EARS AND
HEARTS WITH WISDOM, OUR WORDS
BECOME **A NEVER-ENDING
STREAM OF REFRESHMENT** TO
THOSE AROUND US.

Proverbs 19

PUT THE "US" IN GENEROUS

Everyone loves a generous person. They're just great to be around. Generosity doesn't come naturally to most of us though; it takes work and intentionality. After all, we were born thinking the whole world existed for our benefit. Hang around a baby for just a few minutes and you'll know exactly what I mean. That kid is convinced you and I exist to make his or her life better. "Feed me, clothe me, pay attention to me..." "I'm hot, I'm cold, I'm hungry, I need something but I can't say what it is so I'm just going to scream..." We were born thinking people exist for us so it takes work to shift that mindset.

Never fear! Proverbs 19 is here!

> **"MANY SEEK THE FAVOR OF A GENEROUS MAN, AND EVERYONE IS A FRIEND TO A MAN WHO GIVES GIFTS."**
> **— PROVERBS 19:6 —**

Solomon isn't saying we should attempt to buy friends; he's stating the simple fact that people are drawn to generous people. I don't even know you, but I know you love being around generous people. Since that's the case, we should be generous people! After all, since God has been so generous to us, God's people should be the most generous, loving people on the planet!

> **"GOOD SENSE MAKES ONE SLOW TO ANGER, AND IT IS HIS GLORY TO OVERLOOK AN OFFENSE."**
> **— PROVERBS 19:11 —**

Generosity doesn't only come in the form of physical, tangible gifts. Generosity also happens when we are generous with grace and forgiveness, as God is to us. Overlooking an offense isn't speaking of denial—acting like the offense never happened. Overlooking an offense means dealing with it in its proper context and not blowing it out of proportion. Don't make the repercussions any bigger than they need to be. We should be "slow to anger" and seek to generously forgive the offender.

> "WHOEVER IS GENEROUS TO THE
> POOR LENDS TO THE LORD, AND HE
> WILL REPAY HIM FOR HIS DEED."
> — PROVERBS 19:17 —

There's a simple leadership principle at play here: what is rewarded is repeated. God rewards generosity because He wants us to repeat generosity, especially to the poor. One of the most generous things we can do is give to those who have no capacity to give back. That's a true sign of generosity! It's easy to give when you know you'll get something out of it, but is that really generosity? We should be on the lookout for those in need and be ready and willing to give!

Let's make it our goal to put the "us" back in "generous." Let's reverse the way we entered the world and make our relationships about others instead of about ourselves. A lifestyle of generosity is not only attractive to those who don't know Jesus, but it's also the best, most rewarding way to live!

Dig Deeper

1. Which verse in Proverbs 19 stood out to you most and why?

_____

_____

_____

_____

_____

2. What are some areas of your life where you are stingy and how can you begin to shift them to become areas of generosity?

_____

_____

_____

_____

_____

"

SINCE GOD HAS BEEN SO
GENEROUS TO US, GOD'S PEOPLE
SHOULD BE THE **MOST GENEROUS**,
LOVING PEOPLE ON THE
PLANET!

Proverbs 20

TAKE THE MASK OFF

Every sports team has a mascot that is vital to its brand and brings personality to the team. Have you ever caught one of those mascots after hours, though? Maybe with its head off, smoking a cigarette? It kind of ruins the vibe they've created. Like Buddy the Elf finding out the man at the toy shop isn't the *actual* Santa Claus, finding out their real identity can feel so deflating. The same can happen in a play. An actor on stage wearing a costume and a mask is a different person offstage.

In ancient Roman culture, they had a name for an actor who wore a mask: *hypocrite.*

"Hypocrite" didn't originally have the same negative connotation it has for us today but that's where ours came from. Ultimately, a hypocrite is a person who lacks integrity, someone who is (figuratively) wearing a mask, leading a double life.

Proverbs has some severe warnings against hypocrisy and some wise thoughts about the importance of living with integrity.

> **"THE RIGHTEOUS WHO WALKS IN HIS INTEGRITY—BLESSED ARE HIS CHILDREN AFTER HIM!"**
> **— PROVERBS 20:7 —**

Integrity is honesty. It's being the same person in the spotlight and behind the scenes. It's the opposite of hypocrisy. Integrity takes years to earn and has long-lasting benefits and rewards for our lives. It doesn't only benefit us however—it also benefits the lives of those around us! In the context of parenting, our kids will be better off because of our integrity. The same is also true for other relationships: dating, marriage, close friendships, and even workplace relationships benefit greatly from integrity.

> "WHO CAN SAY, 'I HAVE
> MADE MY HEART PURE; I AM
> CLEAN FROM MY SIN?'"
> — PROVERBS 20:9 —

Integrity is earned, but not entirely. We earn trust from people by proving that we are trustworthy; however, being cleansed of sin is nothing that can be earned. The answer to the rhetorical question of verse 9 is a resounding "no one!" Cleansing from sin is a supernatural work of the Savior.

> "BREAD GAINED BY DECEIT IS SWEET
> TO A MAN, BUT AFTERWARD HIS
> MOUTH WILL BE FULL OF GRAVEL."
> — PROVERBS 20:17 —

Not only does integrity come with a reward, but a lack of integrity comes with a penalty. Nobody wants a mouthful of gravel and although Solomon is using figurative, poetic language here, it captures the point. Deceit will come back to bite you, and in this case, it may break your teeth!

> "DO NOT SAY, 'I WILL REPAY
> EVIL;' WAIT FOR THE LORD,
> AND HE WILL DELIVER YOU."
> — PROVERBS 20:22 —

One of the most freeing aspects of a life of integrity is your freedom from revenge. Vengeance is exhausting, damaging, and binding. As we lash out, thinking we are getting the best of someone else, our own bitterness is actually getting the best of us. When we choose to hold a grudge, we are the ones being held captive. Choose love instead of lashing out and watch God deliver you!

Dig Deeper

1. Which verse in Proverbs 20 stood out to you most and why?

_____

_____

_____

_____

_____

2. We are all aware of areas in our lives we aren't being truthful about because they're often the areas that drain the most energy from us. Identify one of those areas in your life, then write down some practical steps you need to take in order to "take the mask off."

_____

_____

_____

_____

_____

_____

"

WHEN WE CHOOSE TO HOLD A
GRUDGE, WE ARE THE ONES BEING
HELD CAPTIVE. **CHOOSE LOVE
INSTEAD OF LASHING OUT.**

Proverbs 21

THREE MAGICAL WORDS

"You are right."

Those three words are music to our ears. They're magical and a reason to celebrate. We love being right, sometimes to a fault. We'll argue our point until we're blue in the face to make sure we win the argument. Although those three words can only be applied to us *sometimes*, they're 100% true about God *all the time*. Whether we agree with Him or not, God is always right. *Always!*

> "THE KING'S HEART IS A STREAM OF
> WATER IN THE HAND OF THE LORD;
> HE TURNS IT WHEREVER HE WILL."
> — PROVERBS 21:1 —

Not only do we like to be right, we also like to be in control. A king—the person with the most power and control in Bible days—is subject to the control of God Himself. King Solomon recognized that although He wanted to be right, God's way is always best. *Even the king is subject to the King of Kings!*

> "TO DO RIGHTEOUSNESS AND
> JUSTICE IS MORE ACCEPTABLE TO
> THE LORD THAN SACRIFICE."
> — PROVERBS 21:3 —

Since God is righteous, it would only make sense that His people are righteous. In Solomon's day, a sacrifice was how they corrected a sinful error. Although a sacrifice was the prescribed way of honoring God after sinning, God would rather the sacrifice not have to take place to begin with. How do we dodge the sacrifice? *Do the right thing.* Obedience, despite the cost, is always preferred over sin and confession.

> "WHOEVER PURSUES RIGHTEOUSNESS
> AND KINDNESS WILL FIND LIFE,
> RIGHTEOUSNESS, AND HONOR."
> — PROVERBS 21:21 —

You reap what you sow. That is a life principle as well as a Biblical principle (see Galatians 6:9). When we pursue righteousness, we can trust we will find it. This is a simple principle to understand, but it can be challenging to live out. Righteousness and kindness are not the natural things we seek, but they are the things God honors.

> "THE HORSE IS MADE READY FOR THE
> DAY OF BATTLE, BUT THE VICTORY
> BELONGS TO THE LORD."
> — PROVERBS 21:31 —

God's righteousness guarantees the victory. No matter the power of the opposition, we trust that if God is for us, it doesn't matter who is against us (Romans 8:31). We don't trust in the power of the war horse, finances, strategy, social status, or connectedness. God gets the credit for the victory.

"You are right" is always a phrase that can (and should) be said to God. God has always been right and always will be. Be thankful for that, then let your life reflect it in everything you do, trusting Him with every decision and every step. And remember, if you pursue righteousness, you will find it!

1. Which verse in Proverbs 21 stood out to you most and why?

_____

_____

_____

_____

_____

_____

2. Say these three words out loud to the Lord: "YOU ARE RIGHT." Make a list of some things in your life that God has proven Himself to be right about, then take some time to thank Him for each one.

_____

_____

_____

_____

_____

"

GOD'S RIGHTEOUSNESS GUARANTEES
THE VICTORY **NO MATTER THE
POWER OF THE OPPOSITION!**

Proverbs 22

GET IT OUT

I don't mean to gross you out or bring up unwanted memories, but I imagine we've all ended up with something in our food that we didn't want in it. Some people have enough willpower to remove it and eat the food anyway. Others (like yours truly) typically want it remade or a different entree altogether. Whichever camp you're in, there are some things we simply do not want in our food.

Similarly, there are many things we do not want in our lives. Proverbs 22-24 contain proverbs written by an unknown group of men simply known as "the wise" (see Proverbs 22:17). Some scholars believe Solomon collected their words and added them to his collection of proverbs. Regardless of who is writing, their words contain wise insights on some of those things we should avoid.

> **"TRAIN UP A CHILD IN THE WAY HE SHOULD GO; EVEN WHEN HE IS OLD HE WILL NOT DEPART FROM IT."**
> **— PROVERBS 22:6 —**

Training children involves introducing them to many things they will want in their lives (God's Word, prayer, faith). It also involves helping them avoid things that are harmful, physically and spiritually. Keep in mind, although Proverbs 22:6 is Godly parenting wisdom, we cannot save our children. This is not a promise that Godly parenting will lead to Godly kids but it is a wise principle to parent with. Pray for your kids and set the example.

> **"DRIVE OUT A SCOFFER, AND STRIFE WILL GO OUT, AND QUARRELING AND ABUSE WILL CEASE."**
> **— PROVERBS 22:10 —**

"Scoffer" isn't a word we typically use but you know some scoffers. The New Living Translation calls them "mockers" and The Message calls them "troublemakers." Suddenly, you can identify some scoffers now, can't you? Solomon is simply reminding us that these people lead us nowhere good. When the troublemakers leave; strife, quarrelling, and abuse follow them out the door. Troublemakers need love too, though! Don't give up on them, but be careful of their influence.

> "FOLLY IS BOUND UP IN THE HEART OF
> A CHILD, BUT THE ROD OF DISCIPLINE
> DRIVES IT FAR FROM HIM."
> — PROVERBS 22:15 —

While there is a lot of modern debate about spanking children, the Bible doesn't mince words. Our family's "rod of discipline" is called "the spanking spoon" and it has struck healthy fear in the hearts of our children as they've grown up. I won't belabor this point, but make sure to catch the principle: *momentary pain can be used to prevent long-lasting, devastating pain.*

> "MAKE NO FRIENDSHIP WITH A MAN GIVEN
> TO ANGER, NOR GO WITH A WRATHFUL
> MAN, LEST YOU LEARN HIS WAYS AND
> ENTANGLE YOURSELF IN A SNARE."
> — PROVERBS 22:24–25 —

The scoffers are back, but this time in the form of someone with an anger problem. Allowing uncontrolled, angry people to influence us is a snare. You'll end up allowing their anger to increase your anger, trapping you in a destructive pattern of lashing out.

Allow Proverbs 22 to be like the road signs that warn of hazards ahead. Let's learn from the mistakes and the wisdom of those who have gone before us so we don't fall into the same traps.

Dig Deeper

1. Which verse in Proverbs 22 stood out to you most and why?

   _____

   _____

   _____

   _____

   _____

   _____

2. Are there voices you've allowed to speak into your life that are leading you astray? What are some steps you can take to drown out those voices and listen to Godly voices?

   _____

   _____

   _____

   _____

   _____

   _____

"

MOMENTARY PAIN CAN BE
USED TO **PREVENT** LONG-LASTING,
DEVASTATING PAIN.

Proverbs 23

TAKE CONTROL

Within the first month or two of purchasing a new TV, our family lost the remote control. Tragic, I know. We couldn't find it anywhere, but losing the remote control led to an interesting discovery: our TV has controls *on it*! Who knew?!

Remote controls, temperature control, birth control… We love control, don't we? In fact, losing the remote control makes us feel out of control (or at least less in control).

One of the big themes of Proverbs 23 has to do with control. The authors remind us of our need to control our thoughts and desires, as well as pay attention to what we allow to control us.

> "LET NOT YOUR HEART ENVY SINNERS,
> BUT CONTINUE IN THE FEAR OF THE LORD
> ALL THE DAY. SURELY THERE IS A FUTURE,
> AND YOUR HOPE WILL NOT BE CUT OFF."
> – PROVERBS 23:17–18 –

Hebrews 12 reminds us we should be "looking to Jesus, the founder and perfecter of our faith" (Hebrews 12:2). When we stop staring at Jesus and let our eyes drift to those around us, envy can quickly kick in, especially in the age of social media. Social media can be a great tool, but one danger it poses is the door it opens to envy. Social media, as well as much of what we see of people's lives from a distance, is a highlight reel. It's the best moments, the most beautiful sunsets, and the most romanticized, edited, cropped, and filtered photos.

Envy is a contentment killer. When we begin to gaze into the lives of others, noticing only the things that seem to go well in their lives, it seems unfair compared to what we know to be true about our own lives. This is where verse 17 comes in: "continue in the fear of the Lord all the day." For those who fear the Lord, there is a future and a hope!

Get that envy under control!

> "THOSE WHO TARRY LONG OVER WINE; THOSE WHO GO TO TRY MIXED WINE. DO NOT LOOK AT WINE WHEN IT IS RED, WHEN IT SPARKLES IN THE CUP AND GOES DOWN SMOOTHLY... YOU WILL BE LIKE ONE WHO LIES DOWN IN THE MIDST OF THE SEA, LIKE ONE WHO LIES ON THE TOP OF A MAST. 'THEY STRUCK ME,' YOU WILL SAY, 'BUT I WAS NOT HURT; THEY BEAT ME, BUT I DID NOT FEEL IT. WHEN SHALL I AWAKE? I MUST HAVE ANOTHER DRINK.'"
> – PROVERBS 23:30–31, 34–35 –

Speaking of control issues, these final verses in Proverbs 23 paint a really dark picture of those who self-medicate their pain and problems with alcohol. Although the Bible never says not to drink, it does command not to be drunk. Here's a little secret: *the best way to not be drunk is to not drink!*

In the New Testament, Paul writes about the controlling nature of alcohol and how to combat it. He says that instead of being controlled by wine, we should be filled with and controlled by the Holy Spirit (Ephesians 5:18). In other words, don't be controlled by *spirits*; be controlled by *the Spirit*.

At the moment of salvation, the Holy Spirit takes up residence inside Christians (Ephesians 1:13). However, fully surrendering to the Spirit and allowing Him to have full control of every area of our lives is a lifelong process. Keep turning over control. The less we are controlled by ourselves and the things around us, the more we can be led and controlled by the Holy Spirit!

Dig Deeper

1. Which verse in Proverbs 23 stood out to you most and why?

_____

_____

_____

_____

_____

_____

2. Do envy or alcohol cause ongoing control issues in your life? What are some things that are controlling you and how can you surrender them so God can control that part of your life?

_____

_____

_____

_____

_____

"

THE LESS WE ARE CONTROLLED
BY OURSELVES AND THE THINGS
AROUND US, **THE MORE WE CAN
BE LED AND CONTROLLED BY
THE HOLY SPIRIT!**

Proverbs 24

A WEAPON AND REWARD

I remember my first pocket knife. It was a knock off Swiss Army knife my dad bought me for $10 on a trip we took to the Grand Canyon. I couldn't believe my luck. I had always wanted a knife and now I finally had one! What I loved even more though was that this was not just a knife, it was a multitool. It had not one blade but two, pliers, a pop-out toothpick, a file, a mini saw, and lots of other tiny gadgets. Eight-year old Kevin could now brave the wild beasts of the Grand Canyon because I would be prepared for anything that came my way!

In the book of Proverbs, wisdom is a multitool. It's valuable, powerful, and extremely useful in every area of life. Here are a few examples...

> "A WISE MAN IS FULL OF STRENGTH, AND
> A MAN OF KNOWLEDGE ENHANCES HIS
> MIGHT, FOR BY WISE GUIDANCE YOU CAN
> WAGE YOUR WAR, AND IN ABUNDANCE
> OF COUNSELORS THERE IS VICTORY."
> – PROVERBS 24:5–6 –

Wisdom isn't just about knowing a lot of things. There are plenty of unwise, knowledgeable people. Wisdom is about receiving from God and the Godly counselors He places in our lives so we can be strengthened for the task and the trials that lie ahead. Verses 5-6 remind us that wisdom brings strength, might, and eventually victory!

Wisdom isn't found just by reading books; it is unearthed through time with the Lord, ongoing conversations and relationships with God's people, and a constant, humble submission to God's leadership. Life is war and if we will be intentional with surrounding ourselves with an "abundance of counselors," we can rest assured of victory!

> "MY SON, EAT HONEY, FOR IT IS GOOD,
> AND THE DRIPPINGS OF THE HONEYCOMB
> ARE SWEET TO YOUR TASTE. KNOW THAT
> WISDOM IS SUCH TO YOUR SOUL; IF YOU
> FIND IT, THERE WILL BE A FUTURE, AND
> YOUR HOPE WILL NOT BE CUT OFF."
> – PROVERBS 24:13–14 –

These verses remind us that wisdom is not only strength for the battle but a reward to keep us going. In the Bible days, honey was the sweetest thing available to eat. It was the Biblical equivalent of Krispy Kreme. Wisdom gives us the strength to keep going and promises a reward when we arrive at the end. When life is tough and circumstances are heavy, seek the wisdom only God can provide and know this: "there will be a future, and your hope will not be cut off."

Dig Deeper

1. Which verse in Proverbs 24 stood out to you most and why?

_____

_____

_____

_____

_____

_____

2. Wisdom is a weapon and a reward, but what else is it to you? What are some other ways you've seen God's wisdom benefit your life?

_____

_____

_____

_____

_____

_____

"

WISDOM IS NOT ONLY STRENGTH
FOR THE BATTLE BUT A REWARD
TO KEEP US GOING.

Proverbs 25

REFRESHMENTS

I grew up playing baseball. There were a lot of things I enjoyed about baseball: the excitement of the game, scoring the winning run, a diving catch, but at least in the early years, the thing I looked forward to the most was the post-game snacks and refreshments! There's nothing quite like an ice cold Capri Sun after a sweaty baseball game. Once, a parent forgot to bring snacks so they bought everyone slushes at the snack bar. For awhile after that, I hoped every parent forgot snacks!

In Proverbs 25, we are back to hearing from Solomon as he reminds us we don't have to wait around on others for refreshments—*we can be the refreshments!*

> "DO NOT PUT YOURSELF FORWARD IN THE KING'S PRESENCE OR STAND IN THE PLACE OF THE GREAT, FOR IT IS BETTER TO BE TOLD, 'COME UP HERE,' THAN TO BE PUT LOWER IN THE PRESENCE OF A NOBLE."
> – PROVERBS 25:6–7 –

Humility is refreshing. It's so refreshing to be around someone who is humble and others-centered. We have all been around people who are the opposite, constantly talking about themselves, their achievements, and their status. Here in Proverbs 25, King Solomon is speaking from experience. I imagine he had plenty of guests who thought more highly of themselves than they should have, many of whom he had to humble. The principle King Solomon shares with us here should be one we live out everywhere, whether we are among royalty, acquaintances, or friends.

> **"LIKE THE COLD OF SNOW IN THE TIME
> OF HARVEST IS A FAITHFUL MESSENGER
> TO THOSE WHO SEND HIM; HE REFRESHES
> THE SOUL OF HIS MASTERS."**
> **– PROVERBS 25:13 –**

Faithfulness is refreshing. Want to be refreshing to those around you? Be faithful with the tasks they give you. If, like the example given here, your task is delivering a message, be faithful with that message. If your job is doing an unglamorous job, do it like everyone is watching. If your job is on a stage or in a spotlight, understand the privilege of that platform and faithfully fulfill your role.

> **"LIKE COLD WATER TO A THIRSTY SOUL, SO
> IS GOOD NEWS FROM A FAR COUNTRY."**
> **– PROVERBS 25:25 –**

Good news is refreshing. On a hot day under the sun, you know how refreshing a glass of ice water is. As followers of Jesus, we carry the best news into a bad news world. I have met a handful of constantly negative Christians in my day and they always confuse me. I can't understand how people with such great hope can be so negative. It's a contradiction. Be a refreshment to those around you by faithfully carrying the good news.

Wherever you go, whatever you do, and whatever you say, be a refreshment to people around you.

Dig Deeper

1. Which verse in Proverbs 25 stood out to you most and why?

_____

_____

_____

_____

_____

_____

2. In addition to being humble, faithful, and generous with the good news, list some other ways you can be a refreshment to people around you.

_____

_____

_____

_____

_____

"
WHEREVER YOU GO,
WHATEVER YOU DO, AND WHATEVER
YOU S AY, **BE A REFRESHMENT**
TO PEOPLE AROUND YOU.

Proverbs 26

NONSENSICAL

Have you ever searched for your sunglasses while they were on your forehead or scoured the house for your keys while you were holding them in your hand? Have you ever packed a lunch then left it on the kitchen counter or moved aside the the thing you were looking for as you were looking for it? Sometimes we do things that make no sense. "What was the point of that and why did I do it?" we ask ourselves.

Proverbs 26 gives a few good examples of things that don't make sense and there is a lot we can learn from them.

> "ANSWER NOT A FOOL ACCORDING TO HIS FOLLY, LEST YOU BE LIKE HIM YOURSELF. ANSWER A FOOL ACCORDING TO HIS FOLLY, LEST HE BE WISE IN HIS OWN EYES."
> – PROVERBS 26:4–5 –

Does it seem odd to anyone else that these two verses seem to give the opposite advice, back to back? So should we answer a fool according to his folly or not? The answer depends on the person and the situation. Sometimes, ignoring a foolish person is the best thing for you and for them. For instance, when people want to argue on social media, I don't engage them. I've found that when I stoop to that level, verse 4 becomes true of me: I become a fool like the hater trying to troll me. However, there is a time and a place to answer someone according to their foolishness. After all, there are certain times we could all benefit from a loving rebuke.

> "LIKE A DOG THAT RETURNS TO HIS VOMIT IS A FOOL WHO REPEATS HIS FOLLY."
> – PROVERBS 26:11 –

This is a disgusting illustration, but if you've been around dogs long enough, you've witnessed it. Unfortunately, we can be similarly guilty of repeating the same foolish actions over and over again. It's nonsensical. It's the struggle Paul addresses in Romans 7, where he describes the internal battle between right and wrong. The things he wants to do he doesn't do, and the things he doesn't want to do, he does. We need to daily rely on the power of God at work in our lives in order to break this cycle of foolishness.

> "FOR LACK OF WOOD THE FIRE
> GOES OUT, AND WHERE THERE IS NO
> WHISPERER, QUARRELING CEASES."
> – PROVERBS 26:20 –

Speaking of powerful visuals, here's one! Whispering, or gossipping, in this verse is related to throwing wood on a fire. When we whisper behind people's backs, we're fueling the fire. It doesn't make sense for us to do that. We need to remember the power of our words and choose to use them for good, not for destruction.

It's time to take a stand against the things in our lives we know we shouldn't be doing. It's not an easy fight, but it's a worthwhile fight.

Dig Deeper

1. Which verse in Proverbs 26 stood out to you most and why?

_____

_____

_____

_____

_____

_____

2. Think about some weak areas in your life where you are commonly going back to foolish or harmful actions. What are some ways you can begin to break that cycle?

_____

_____

_____

_____

_____

_____

"

REMEMBER THE POWER OF
OUR WORDS AND CHOOSE
TO USE THEM FOR GOOD,
NOT FOR DESTRUCTION.

Proverbs 27

THE HARD TRUTH

The truth hurts. You've probably heard someone tell you that and you've definitely experienced it. Sometimes, no matter how sugar-coated the truth may be, it can still be hard to swallow. When it comes to the Bible, one of the many things I'm thankful for is its loving, honest approach to the truth. Below are some (non-candy-coated) truths to chew on.

> "DO NOT BOAST ABOUT TOMORROW, FOR YOU
> DO NOT KNOW WHAT A DAY MAY BRING."
> – PROVERBS 27:1 –

Hard truth: the future is much more mysterious than you wish it was.

Whether we like it or not, we don't know a whole lot about the future. In reality, the only thing we know for sure are the names of the upcoming days and months. Science has helped us predict weather patterns and moon phases, but even those are just educated guesses. Some people obsess over knowing the future and will go to great lengths through astrology, fortune telling, ouija boards, and more to reveal the future. As much as we think we want to know the details of the future, one of the ways God demonstrates His love for us is by concealing many of those details. If we knew all the forthcoming details, they would immobilize us for what we should be focused on right now. *You don't have to know the future when you know Who holds it!*

> "FAITHFUL ARE THE WOUNDS OF A FRIEND;
> PROFUSE ARE THE KISSES OF AN ENEMY."
> – PROVERBS 27:6 –

Hard truth: wounds will happen and although they hurt, sometimes they are helpful.

Wounds are never fun, but they can be delivered faithfully. Wounds are faithful when they are inflicted by a friend in order to help you, not to hurt you. Think of it like surgery. You wouldn't be mad at a surgeon for cutting you open to remove a tumor, but still, he wounded you. In the context of surgery, the wound is given in order to bring healing. That's exactly what a friend does. A Godly friend doesn't just say what you want to hear; they are willing to risk the pain of saying what needs to be said in order to help you. It's been said that *a Godly friend doesn't stab you in the back; they stab you in the front.* As we grow in our faith and surround ourselves with Godly, truth-telling friends, we'll learn to be thankful for those loving stab wounds.

> "WHOEVER BLESSES HIS NEIGHBOR WITH
> A LOUD VOICE, RISING EARLY IN THE
> MORNING, WILL BE COUNTED AS CURSING."
> – PROVERBS 27:14 –

I'll just leave that right there as a warning to all the early risers and as an encouragement to all the later sleepers!

> "THE CRUCIBLE IS FOR SILVER, AND
> THE FURNACE IS FOR GOLD, AND A
> MAN IS TESTED BY HIS PRAISE."
> – PROVERBS 27:21 –

The praise of people can make or break you. The outcome depends on what you do with it and what you allow it to do to you. According to this verse, when people praise us, it's a test. How will we respond? Will you allow it to go to your head and inflate your ego or will you allow it to humble you, making you grateful for how God is using you? Your ego is not your amigo, so be extra cautious when you feel it growing. It can take over quicker than you imagine!

1. Which verse in Proverbs 27 stood out to you most and why?

_____

_____

_____

_____

_____

_____

2. Of the hard truths we discussed from Proverbs 27, which is the hardest for you to swallow and why?

_____

_____

_____

_____

_____

_____

"

THE PRAISE OF PEOPLE CAN
MAKE OR BREAK YOU. THE OUTCOME
DEPENDS ON WHAT YOU DO WITH
IT AND **WHAT YOU ALLOW
IT TO DO TO YOU.**

Proverbs 28

BOLDNESS FOR THE BATTLE

Life is war. There's no need to dance around the obvious. If you're a follower of Jesus, the Devil wants you down for the count. We shouldn't expect a standing ovation from the demonic realm when we choose to obey God and walk by faith.

Thankfully Proverbs 28 provides some great wisdom on how to confidently face the battle as well as some areas we need to be confident in. Lean in as we hear from Solomon on the topic.

> **"THE WICKED FLEE WHEN NO ONE PURSUES,**
> **BUT THE RIGHTEOUS ARE BOLD AS A LION."**
> **– PROVERBS 28:1 –**

Since those who don't know God have no foundation for their lives or beliefs, life tends to be lived in flight mode, always on the run. Although no one is pursuing, they're running. The righteous, on the other hand, are as bold as a lion. Have you ever seen a lion cower in fear? Of course not. They face the opposition, whether it is another lion or a different predator, with frightening boldness. What a great picture of how a follower of Jesus should live! Since our foundation is built on Jesus, the chief cornerstone (1 Peter 2:6), it should not matter who or what is against us since He is for us (Romans 8:31). Walk in confidence knowing that He who is in you is greater than he who is in the world (1 John 4:4). Go get 'em...*lion*!

> **"BETTER IS A POOR MAN WHO WALKS**
> **IN HIS INTEGRITY THAN A RICH MAN**
> **WHO IS CROOKED IN HIS WAYS."**
> **– PROVERBS 28:6 –**

The New Testament defines integrity as living "above reproach," living in a way that slander doesn't stick. Honestly, living without integrity often appears easier. In the moment, it feels easier to cut corners, slander others, bypass rules, or tell a lie here and there. Although integrity *requires* boldness to do it the right way, integrity also *produces* boldness. When we are living a life of integrity, there is no need for us to be constantly looking over our shoulders, wondering if we'll be caught, or keeping track of who we told which lie to. Consistently do the right thing and your life will be better and bolder for it. All the money in the world can't purchase a clean conscience or the confidence that comes from a life of integrity.

> "WHOEVER CONCEALS HIS TRANSGRESSIONS
> WILL NOT PROSPER, BUT HE WHO CONFESSES
> AND FORSAKES THEM WILL OBTAIN MERCY."
> – PROVERBS 28:13 –

Although our aim should be to consistently walk in obedience and do the right thing, the reality is that we will fail. How we respond to failure is very important. If we deny our failure, we won't learn from it, and we can actually develop a dangerous habit of denial. However, if we choose to confess and forsake (both are important), we can rest in God's mercy and mercy from others. By the way, when you finally decide to come out of the shadows and confess your sin, chances are, people won't be nearly as shocked as you think they will be. In fact, when you speak up, it may just give someone else the courage they need to speak up, setting in motion a chain reaction of honesty and freedom!

Dig Deeper

1. Which verse in Proverbs 28 stood out to you most and why?

_____

_____

_____

_____

_____

2. Think through some areas in your life that you lack boldness in. It could be doing the right thing, confessing sin, boldness in parenting, sharing your faith, etc. As you make a list of those things, put a plan in place on how you can increase your boldness in those areas.

_____

_____

_____

_____

_____

"

ALTHOUGH INTEGRITY
REQUIRES BOLDNESS, **IT ALSO
PRODUCES BOLDNESS.**

𝔓𝔯𝔬𝔳𝔢𝔯𝔟𝔰 29

IT'S A TRAP!

We've all seen news stories of huge sinkholes that opened up after a storm. Clarksville has been home to a few of them. In fact, a sinkhole on our college football field even made national news! Thankfully, whenever a sinkhole opens, there are immediate precautions taken. Roads are closed and barriers are erected, all so danger can be averted. It would be dangerous and wrong to know about the potential hazard and do nothing to prevent people from harm.

Proverbs 29 gives us some blaring signals, warning us of danger that lies ahead.

> "HE WHO IS OFTEN REPROVED, YET
> STIFFENS HIS NECK, WILL SUDDENLY
> BE BROKEN BEYOND HEALING."
> – PROVERBS 29:1 –

A stiff neck will eventually become a broken neck. No one likes reproof or correction, but it is necessary for our growth and well-being. We need guidance and as Proverbs has reminded us time and again, if we surround ourselves with the right people and listen to the right voices, we'll be better for it. Although we may know reproof is for our good, if we get in the habit of resisting it, it can lead to tragedy. I've personally known people—even close friends—who have thrown their lives and callings away because they stubbornly insisted on doing things their own way. Don't do it. *It's a trap!*

> "A MAN WHO FLATTERS HIS NEIGHBOR
> SPREADS A NET FOR HIS FEET."
> – PROVERBS 29:5 –

Flattery means saying nice things to get what you want. If we get in the habit of it, we set a trap for ourselves. This is not saying to bad-mouth people just because what you are saying is true. As your mother may have told you, "Just because it's true doesn't mean you need to say it." Verse 5 is simply a reminder that flattery is a disservice to ourselves as well as to others. It's dishonest and does not provide the honest feedback necessary for their growth. Don't flatter. *It's a trap!*

> ## "A FOOL GIVES FULL VENT TO HIS SPIRIT, BUT A WISE MAN QUIETLY HOLDS IT BACK."
> ### – PROVERBS 29:11 –

Next time someone you know starts off on a rant and says they just need to vent, pull out Proverbs 29:11. Actually, on second thought, don't. Mid-rant is probably not the right time. However, next time you're tempted to "let someone have it" because "they had it coming" (or whatever justification or rationale you choose), think twice. Wisdom stays quiet when foolishness would lash out. Don't rant and rave. *It's a trap!*

> ## "THE FEAR OF MAN LAYS A SNARE, BUT WHOEVER TRUSTS IN THE LORD IS SAFE."
> ### – PROVERBS 29:25 –

The fear of man and trust in the Lord are mutually exclusive. You can't fear man while also trusting in the Lord, and vice versa. It's one or the other. The choice is yours. You can either do one that is a snare or the other that keeps you safe. Although the choice seems relatively simple when put in black and white like that, choosing to trust the Lord can be very challenging. No matter how hard, do it anyway. *Living in the fear of man is a trap!*

Dig Deeper

1. Which verse in Proverbs 29 stood out to you most and why?

_____

_____

_____

2. Do you tend to live more in the fear of men or trust in the Lord?

_____

_____

_____

_____

3. What are some ways you can learn to trust God and live in that trust even more?

_____

_____

_____

_____

"

THE FEAR OF MAN AND TRUST IN
THE LORD ARE MUTUALLY EXCLUSIVE.
YOU CAN'T FEAR MAN WHILE ALSO
TRUSTING IN THE LORD.

Proverbs 30

LISTEN MORE, TALK LESS

The book of Proverbs provides hundreds of wise sayings from King Solomon and a few other "wise men."

Proverbs 30 is written by Agur son of Jakeh. Interestingly, we know nothing of Agur or Jakeh besides what is written in this Proverb. Theories abound on Agur's identity, but nothing is for sure. What we do know is that he was wise, intuitive, and inquisitive. It's also interesting to note that even if Proverbs didn't tell us this chapter was written by someone else, you would be able to tell just by reading it. It reads different, sounds different, and is even composed differently. I'm thankful God speaks *through* people and not *despite* people. He uses our God-given personality and style to speak *to* and *through* us.

> "EVERY WORD OF GOD PROVES TRUE; HE IS
> A SHIELD TO THOSE WHO TAKE REFUGE IN
> HIM. DO NOT ADD TO HIS WORDS, LEST HE
> REBUKE YOU AND YOU BE FOUND A LIAR."
> – PROVERBS 30:5–6 –

Obviously, there's no way to write down everything in human history that has ever happened or every single answer to every question we will have. God's Word is unapologetically the spiritual "Cliffs Notes" for life. It provides basic wisdom and overarching principles that cover every area of life. This is why Peter can say, "His divine power has granted to us all things that pertain to life and godliness" (2 Peter 1:3). We need to trust that He has given us everything we need. There are many things God purposely has not told us. We need to learn to take Him at His word, resting in the truth that "every word of God proves true." Don't give into the temptation to add anything to what He has already said. He's given us what we need, so let's listen more and trust God with everything we have.

> **"IF YOU HAVE BEEN FOOLISH, EXALTING YOURSELF, OR IF YOU HAVE BEEN DEVISING EVIL, PUT YOUR HAND ON YOUR MOUTH."**
> **– PROVERBS 30:32 –**

"Put your hand on your mouth" may be some of the most honest, practical, and wise advice the Bible gives! Thank you, Agur son of Jakeh. After questioning his existence and God's goodness, Job learned this the hard way, then followed through with the "hand-on-mouth" advice (see Job 40:4). As Proverbs comes to a close and we think through what we've been learning, I think this advice is even more practical. Let's learn to stop exalting ourselves and devising evil, which we've learned are both traps, and instead, listen more. Let's listen to others, and most importantly, listen to God.

Since God's Word always proves true, we can confidently trust that as He speaks and we listen, our lives will be better for it.

Dig Deeper

1. Which verse in Proverbs 30 stood out to you most and why?

_____

_____

_____

2. What are some ways your life and the lives of others would benefit from you listening more and speaking less?

_____

_____

_____

3. What are some practical ways you can be better at listening more and speaking less?

_____

_____

_____

_____

"

SINCE GOD'S WORD ALWAYS
PROVES TRUE, WE CAN CONFIDENTLY
TRUST THAT AS HE SPEAKS AND
WE LISTEN, **OUR LIVES WILL BE
BETTER FOR IT.**

$\mathfrak{Proverbs}$ 31

WONDER WOMAN

Although we know very little about the author of Proverbs 31, King Lemuel, it may be one of the best known Proverbs. It's a huge compliment to refer to a woman as a "Proverbs 31 Woman," as you'll see as you read through this final chapter.

Instead of hearing from a male perspective on this chapter, I wanted you to hear from a Godly female. I chose someone who embodies this chapter in her marriage, her parenting, and how she walks out her faith: *my wife, Jenn!* Here are some wise words from Jenn, on Proverbs 31.

The "Proverbs 31 woman" is someone we have probably all heard about. It appears, as you read through this chapter, that a more appropriate name for the Proverbs 31 Woman is "Wonder Woman." It seems as though she can do *all* things and that she does them all well. However, this chapter is not about perfection, it's really all about making progress. I think we all know that perfection is not really attainable because ultimately we're human and until heaven, nothing about us will be perfect. However, we can all make progress (men and women) as we pursue the Perfect One.

Here are a few things I learned about the Proverbs 31 woman:

- *She honors her husband (verse 12)*
- *She is diligent in all she does (verses 13-14, 19)*
- *She is not lazy (verses 15, 18, 27)*
- *She serves extravagantly (verse 20)*
- *She is not ruled by fear (verses 21, 25)*
- *She is confident (verse 25)*
- *Her words are filled with wisdom and kindness (verse 26)*

These characteristics are good, but how do we get them? Verse 30 is our answer:

> "CHARM IS DECEITFUL, AND BEAUTY
> IS VAIN, BUT A WOMAN WHO *FEARS*
> *THE LORD* IS TO BE PRAISED."
> – PROVERBS 31:30 –

Fearing the Lord should be our first priority. When we worship, obey, serve, and trust Him with an awe-filled respect, the characteristics that describe the Proverbs 31 woman will be true of us. *However*, don't expect this to happen overnight. It will take time, effort, and perseverance. We can show up to church on Sunday, hear the word of God, sing a few songs, and serve in a ministry, but what about the rest of the week? Fearing the Lord doesn't just happen one day a week or when it's convenient for you. Fearing God is a daily choice and begins with spending time in His Word getting to know Him.

One way we may miss out on becoming a woman (or man) who fears the Lord is by neglecting God's Word. Psalm 19 tells us that God's Word should be desired more than anything and it is sweeter than any words (or food) you'll ever hear (or eat)!

When the Word of God is at work within you, the work of God will flow through you.

Oftentimes, the way God works through us is by the very characteristics we acquire as we pursue Him. Let your work ethic, your diligence in your school work, the way you serve, what you say, how you treat people, and all that you do, point back to the fact that you are a woman (or man) who fears the Lord!

Dig Deeper

1. Which verse in Proverbs 31 stood out to you most and why?

_____

_____

_____

2. As you read through some of the characteristics of a Godly woman, which ones come easier to you and which ones require more intentionality?

_____

_____

_____

3. If God's Word is at work within you, how is His Word flowing out of you?

_____

_____

_____

_____

"

WHEN THE WORD OF GOD
IS AT WORK WITHIN YOU, **THE
WORK OF GOD WILL FLOW
THROUGH YOU.**

About the Authors

Kevin and Jenn Miller grew up in Albuquerque, New Mexico and a few surrounding cities. They even attended some of the same concerts and events, but didn't meet until after high school. They both gave their lives to Jesus at a young age and were raised going to church. Jenn began leading worship at the age of thirteen and became highly involved with youth ministry. When Kevin was sixteen years old, he was involved in helping launch a student-run youth group at his church and began teaching a weekly Bible study at his high school. Four years later, a year and a half after he and Jenn met, they were married and Kevin was hired as the Middle School Youth Pastor at Calvary Church in Albuquerque. After five years on staff, Kevin and Jenn, along with their two-year-old daughter, and some friends, moved from Albuquerque to Clarksville, TN to plant Awaken Church in 2009.

Jenn leads Revive, a ministry of Awaken Church, which is a monthly gathering of ladies. She teaches Revive monthly and has had opportunities to speak to large and small audiences at retreats, events, conferences, and more. Kevin preaches weekly at Awaken Church and has also had many opportunities to speak to large and small groups at churches, conferences, events, classes, and other gatherings both around the United States and in other countries. Kevin and Jenn live in Clarksville, TN and have three children: Emery, Adalyn, and Haddon.

About Awaken Church

In the summer of 2009, a team of five (Pastor Kevin and Jenn Miller, Pastor Nate and Jenn Witiuk, and their friend Denver Miller) uprooted their lives from Albuquerque, NM to plant Awaken Church. They began with simple park outreaches, which grew into a home Bible study and eventually led them to Riverside Center. The team had been in Clarksville for less than three months when Awaken opened its doors on September 19, 2009 and one person accepted Christ on the very first night!

The church grew to about 25 adults in the first eight months when a rainstorm hit in May 2010. That storm caused major flooding, destroying 144 businesses on Riverside Drive, including Awaken Church. After the flood, Awaken owned less than when the moving trucks had first rolled into Clarksville.

Although the flood was devastating, God used it to provide for the church in unexpected ways. They relocated, renovated, and relaunched, becoming one of the first Riverside businesses to reopen. They quickly outgrew their renovated space, leading to their move across the parking lot to a space that was twice the size. They quickly grew into the new space, while adding services and additional square footage to accommodate the continued growth.

In December 2013, Awaken opened its second venue, right in Riverside Center, allowing them to double their seating capacity at each service. Not long after that, right after the church turned five years old, they purchased the entire Riverside Center shopping center!

Over the years, Awaken has given away hundreds of thousands of dollars by partnering both locally and globally with organizations such as: Hope Pregnancy Center, Manna Cafe, Child Evangelism Fellowship, Restoring the Warrior's Heart, XXXchurch, Faith Comes By Hearing, Samaritan's Purse, American Cancer Society, ARC, The Exodus Road, YouVersion Bible app, as well as other churches and church plants.

Through weekend services and outreach events like Good Friday, Easter, The Uprising, Vivid, and more, Awaken Church has celebrated hundreds of faith decisions and a global impact through online streaming.

WE NEVER STOP.

If Jesus hasn't returned and our lungs still have breath in them, we refuse to sit back, slow down, or give up. We will keep going until every person has heard about Jesus.

Acknowledgements

Jenn Miller, my incredible wife: Thank you for writing chapter 31 and for being a Godly woman who fears the Lord. I pray I am the Proverbs 31:28 husband who constantly praises you. You deserve it!

Ellie Tackett: Your creative eye, layout and design skills, and relentless attention to detail make this book one I want to constantly look at. You crushed it.

Richard Cozby: You have the photo skillz to pay the billz. Thanks for your creative eye and photography wizardry.

Tiffany Rockhold: Thank you for spending hours and hours reading, researching, editing, tweaking, and making this book sound as good as it looks.

Tina Medina: Thank you for coordinating this collaborative project, keeping us on schedule, and removing the extra 768 commas I tried to include. Here are a few leftovers:,,,,,,,,,,

Nate Witiuk: Thank you for the idea to turn these daily blog posts into a devotional book.

Pastors Frank Ramseur, Nate Witiuk, Skip Heitzig, and Chris Norman: Thank you for preaching in my absence during this message series. Your voices into my life and our church are God-given and filled with wisdom.

Janice Jenkins: Thanks for working so hard to distill my words down into bite-size email posts, making the words of this book accessible to many more people.

Jacob Vicars: Thank you for burning the midnight oil getting the website up and ready for the world to see.

Breezy Krueger: Thank you for allowing us to unexpectedly rope you into 48 hours of reading and proofing this book! Good work.

Thank YOU for reading this book, and most importantly, reading God's Word. On behalf of the *Better Than Gold* team at Awaken Church, we pray you have experienced the gold mine of God's Word and you never stop going back to it!

CONNECT WITH KEVIN

KEVMILL.COM

VISIT THE
BETTER THAN GOLD WEBSITE

AWAKEN.CHURCH/BETTERTHANGOLD

TO VIEW OUR TEACHINGS AND
DOWNLOAD SERIES ARTWORK.

Printed in the United States
By Bookmasters